Santa Paws

Nicholas Edwards

Hippo

Scholastic Children's Books,
Commonwealth House, 1–19 New Oxford Street,
London WC1A 1NU, UK
a division of Scholastic Ltd
London ~ New York ~ Toronto ~ Sydney ~ Auckland

First published in the USA by Scholastic Inc., 1995
First published in the UK by Scholastic Ltd, 1996

Text copyright © Ellen Emerson White, 1995

ISBN 0 590 19045 8

Typeset by TW Typesetting, Midsomer Norton, Avon

Printed by Cox & Wyman Ltd, Reading, Berks.

10 9 8 7 6 5 4 3 2 1

Chapter 1

When the dog woke up, it was very cold. On winter nights, his mother always brought him, along with his brother and sisters, to some safe place out of the wind. She would scratch up some dry leaves to make them a little nest, and they would all cuddle up together. Then, in the morning, his mother would go off and try to find food for them. Sometimes she would let them come along, although they were too small to be much help. Mostly, she would forage for food while he and his siblings would scuffle and play somewhere nearby.

Once, his mother had lived in a big, nice house with a lot of college students. But then, when it got warm, they all left. She wasn't sure why they hadn't wanted her to come with them. Some of the students had even left without patting her, or saying goodbye. Her favourite, Jason, had filled up her water dish, given her some biscuits and told her what a good dog she was. But then, he got in his car and drove away, too.

She had waited in front of the house for a long time, but none of them came back. Ever since then, she had lived on the streets. Sometimes, nice people would give her food, but more often, she was on her own. There were even times when people would be mean and throw things at her, or chase her away.

Then, when he and his siblings were born, she had to spend most of her time taking care of them. She had a special route of rubbish bins and other places she would check for discarded food. If she found anything, like stale bread or old doughnuts, she would drag the food back and they would all gobble it down. On special days, she might even find some meat in funny plastic packages. They would tear them open and gulp down the old hamburger or bacon or chicken. He and his siblings would always fight playfully over the last little bits, but when his mother growled at them, they would stop right away and be good. The days when she brought home meat were the best days of all. Too often though, when they went to sleep, they were all still very hungry.

He was the smallest of the four puppies, but he had the biggest appetite and slept the most, too. Lots of mornings, he would wake up and be the only one left under the abandoned porch, or in a deep gully, or wherever they had spent the night. Lately, they had been sleeping in an old forgotten shed, behind a house where no people lived. It was safer that way. Lots of times, even if they wagged their tails, people would yell at them or act afraid. But when he saw big scary cars speed by, with happy dogs looking out the windows, he wished he knew *those* people. He also liked the people who would saunter down the street, with dogs on leashes walking proudly next to them. He really wanted to *be* one of those lucky dogs.

But, he wasn't, and he was happy, anyway. His mother always took care of them, and he loved his brother and sisters. They were a family, and as long as they were together, they were safe.

On this particular morning, he yawned a few times, and then rolled to his feet. None of the others were around, but he was sure they would be back soon with some breakfast. Maybe today they would even find some meat! Once he had stood up, he stretched a few times and yawned again. It was *really* cold, and he shivered a little. In fact, it would be nice to curl up again and get some more sleep. But he decided that he was more thirsty than he was sleepy and that it was time to go outside.

There was a hole in the back part of the old shed that they used for a door. He squirmed through it and immediately felt ice-cold snow under his paws. He shivered again, and shook the snow off each paw. It was *much* windier outside than it had been in the shed and he stepped tentatively through the fresh drifts of snow.

In the woods nearby, there was a small stream, where they would always drink. On some mornings lately, the water would be frozen, but his mother had shown him how to stamp his paw on the ice to break it. Today, there was so much snow that he couldn't even *find* the water at first. Then, when he did, he couldn't break the ice. He jumped with all four feet, slipping and sliding, but nothing happened. The ice was just too thick. Finally, he gave up and sat down in the snow, whimpering a little. Now he was going to be hungry *and* thirsty.

He swallowed a few mouthfuls of snow, but he still felt thirsty. The snow also made his insides feel cold. Where was his mother? Where were his brother and sisters? They had never left him for such a long time before. He ran back and forth in front of the frozen stream, whining anxiously. What if they were lost? What if they were hurt? What if they *never* came back? What would happen to him?

Maybe they were back at the shed, waiting for him. Maybe they had brought back food, and he and his brother could roll and play and pretend to fight over it. He should have waited for them, instead of wandering away.

He ran through the woods to the shed. Some of the snowdrifts were so tall that they were almost over his head and it took a lot of energy to bound through them. No, they would never go away and forget him. Never, ever.

But the shed was still deserted. He barked a few times, then waited for answering barks. Lately, his bark had been getting bigger and deeper, so he filled his chest with air and tried again. His bark echoed loudly through the silent backyard and woods. When there was still no answer, he whimpered and lay down to wait for them.

He rested his head on his numb front paws. They would probably come back through the big field behind the shed, and he watched the empty acres miserably. If he moved, he might miss them, so he would just stay here and wait. No matter how long it took, he would stay.

The sun was out and shining on him, which made him feel better. He waited patiently, staring at the field with his ears pricked forward alertly. He could hear birds, and squirrels, and faraway cars – but no dogs. He lifted his nose to try and catch their scent in the air, but he couldn't smell them, either.

So, he just waited. And waited, and waited, and waited. The sun went away after a while, and dark grey clouds rolled in to cover the sky. But still, he waited.

A light snow started falling, but he didn't abandon his post. He wanted to be able to *see* his family the second they came back. Every so often he would stand up to shake off the fresh flakes of snow that had landed on his fur. Then he would shiver, stamp out a new bed for himself, and lie back down. He had never felt so cold, and lonely, and miserable in his life.

Once it began to get dark, he couldn't help whimpering some more and yelping a few times. Something very bad must have happened to his family. Maybe, instead of waiting so long, he should have tried to follow their trail. Maybe they were hurt somewhere, or trapped. But if he went to look for them, they might come back while he was gone and think *he* was lost for good. Then they might go away and he would *never* find them.

There was a street running in front of the boarded-up house and a car was cruising slowly by. A bright beam of light flashed across the house and yard. The dog cringed and tried to duck out of the way. His mother had taught them that when people came around, it was usually safer to hide, just in case.

The car braked to a stop and two big men in uniforms got out. They were both local police officers, out on their nightly patrol.

"Come on, Steve," the man who had been driving said, as he stood by the squad car. "I didn't see anything."

Steve, who was about thirty years old with thick dark hair, aimed his torch around the yard. "We've had three break-ins in the last week," he answered. "If we have drifters in town, this is the kind of place where they might hide out."

"I know," the other cop, who was named Bill, said, sounding defensive. He was heavier than Steve was, with thinning blond hair and a neatly trimmed moustache. "I went to the academy, too, remember?"

Steve grinned at him. "Well, yeah, Bill," he agreed. "But *I* studied."

Bill laughed and snapped on his own torch. "OK, fair enough," he said, and directed the beam at the boarded-up windows of the house. "But, come on. Oceanport isn't exactly a high crime area."

"Law and order," Steve said cheerfully. "That's our job, pal."

The men sounded friendly, but the dog uneasily hung back in the shadows. One of the lights passed over him, paused, and came whipping back.

"There!" Steve said, and pointed towards the shed. "I told you I saw something!"

"Whoa, a *dog*," Bill said, his voice a little sarcastic. "We'd better call for back-up."

Steve ignored him and walked further into the yard. "It must be one of those strays," he said. "I thought Charlie finally managed to round all of them up this morning." Charlie was the animal control officer in Oceanport.

Bill shrugged. "So, he missed one. We'll

put a report in, and he can come back out here tomorrow."

"It's *cold*," Steve said. "You really want to leave the poor thing out here all night? He looks like he's only a puppy."

Bill made a face. "I don't feel like chasing around after him in the snow, either. Let Charlie do it. He needs the exercise."

Steve crouched down, holding his gloved hand out. "Come here, boy! Come on, pup!"

The dog hung back. What did they want? Should he go over there, or run away and hide? His mother would know. He whined quietly and kept his distance.

"He's wild, Steve," Bill said. "This'll take all night."

Steve shook his head, still holding his hand out. "Charlie said they were just scared. He figured once the vet checked them over and they got a few decent meals, they'd be fine." He snapped his fingers. "Come here, boy. Come on."

The dog shifted his weight and stayed where he was. He had to be careful. It might be some kind of trap.

"He's pretty mangy-looking," Bill said critically.

Steve frowned at him. "Are you kidding? That dog's at least half German shepherd. Clean him up a little, and he'd be something to see. And he's young, too. He'd be easy to train."

Bill looked dubious. "Maybe. Give me a good retriever, any day."

Steve stood up abruptly. "Wait a minute. I've got an idea. I still have a sandwich in the car."

"I'm starved," Bill said, trailing after him. "Don't give it to the dog, give it to *me*."

Steve paid no attention. He dug into a brown paper bag below the front seat of the squad car and pulled out a thick, homemade sandwich wrapped in greaseproof paper. "If I catch him, can you take him home?" he asked.

"Are you serious? You know how tough my cat is," Bill said. "Besides, you're the one who likes him so much."

"Yeah," Steve agreed, "but I can't keep him. Not with Emily due any day now. I don't want to do anything to upset her. Besides, she's *already* bugged about me not getting the lights on the Christmas tree yet."

"You'd better get moving," Bill said, laughing. "There's only a week to go."

Steve nodded wryly. "I know, I know. I'm going to do it tomorrow, before my shift – I swear."

As he crossed the yard, carrying the sandwich, the dog shrank away from him. After all, it *could* be some kind of trick. His mother always helped him decide who they could trust, and who they couldn't. He didn't know *how* to take care of himself.

"Hey, what about your brother?" Bill suggested. "Didn't he have to have that old collie of his put to sleep recently?"

"Yeah, a few weeks ago," Steve said, and held the sandwich out in the dog's direction. "My niece and nephew are still heartbroken."

Bill shrugged. "So, bring the dog to them."

Steve thought about that, then shook his head. "I don't know, you can't force a thing like that. They might not be ready yet."

Just then, the police radio in their squad car crackled. They both straightened up and listened, as the dispatcher called in a burglar alarm in their sector.

"Looks like the dog is going to have to wait," Bill said. He hurried over to the car and picked up the radio to report in.

Steve gazed across the dark yard at the shivering little dog. "I'm sorry, pal," he said. "We'll send Charlie out after you tomorrow. Try to stay warm tonight." Gently, he set the meatloaf sandwich down in the snow. "Enjoy your supper now." Then he walked quickly back to the car.

The dog waited right where he was, even after the police car was gone. Then, tentatively, he took a couple of steps out of the woods. He hesitated, sniffed the air, and hesitated some more. Finally, he got up his nerve and bolted across the yard. He was so hungry that he gobbled each sandwich half in two huge bites, and then licked the surrounding snow for any crumbs he might have missed.

It was the best meal he had had for a long time.

Once he was finished, he ran back to the shed and wiggled inside through the hole in the back. If he waited all night, maybe his family would come back. No matter what, he would stay on guard until they did. He was very tired, but he would *make* himself stay awake.

The night before, he and his family had slept in a tangle of leaves and an old musty tarpaulin. The shed had felt crowded, but very warm and safe.

Tonight, all the dog felt was afraid, and very, very alone.

Chapter 2

It was a long cold night, and even though he tried as hard as he could to remain on guard, the dog finally fell asleep. When he woke up in the grey dawn light, he was still alone. His family really *had* left him!

He crept over to the jagged wooden hole in the back of the shed and peeked outside. Even more snow had fallen during the night, and the whole world looked white and scary. Just as he started to put his front paws through the hole, he heard a small truck parking on the street. Instantly, he retreated.

It was Charlie Norris, who was the animal control officer for the small town of Ocean-port. He climbed out of his truck, with some dog biscuits in one hand, and a specially designed noose-like leash in the other.

Inside the shed, the dog could hear the man trampling around through the snow, whistling and calling out, "Here, boy!" But the dog didn't move, afraid of what the man might do to him. The biscuits smelled good, but the leash looked dangerous. He *wanted* to go outside, but if the man tried to take him away, he would miss his family when they came back to get him.

"Don't see any footprints," the man mumbled to himself as he wandered around the snowy yard. "Guess the poor little thing took off last night." He looked around some more, then finally gave up and went back to his truck.

After the truck had driven away, the dog ventured outside. Today, he was going to go and *look* for his family. No more waiting. First, he lifted his leg to mark a couple of spots near the shed. That way, if they came back, they would know that he hadn't gone far.

He stuck his muzzle in the wind, and then down in the snow. With the new drifts, it was hard to pick up a scent. But he found a faint whiff and began following it.

The trail led him through the woods, in the opposite direction from the frozen stream. A couple of times, he lost the scent and had to snuffle around in circles to pick it up again.

Then, he came to a wide road and lost the trail completely. He ran back and forth, sniffing frantically. The smells of exhaust fumes and motor oil were so strong that they covered up everything else. He whined in frustration and widened his search, but the trail was gone.

He galloped across the street, and sharp crystals of road salt and gravel cut into his paws. He limped the rest of the way and plunged into the mammoth drifts on the other side. Again, he ran in wide circles, trying to pick up the trail.

It was no use. His family was *gone*.

He was on his own.

He ran back to where he had first lost the scent, his paws stinging again from the road salt. He searched some more, but the trail just plain disappeared. Finally, he gave up and lay down in the spot where his family had last been.

He stayed there, curled into an unhappy ball, for a very long time. Cars drove by, now and then, but no one noticed him huddled up behind the huge bank of snow.

Finally, he rose stiffly to his feet. His joints felt achy and frozen from the cold. He had tried to lick the salt from his paws to stop the burning, but the terrible taste only made him more thirsty. He needed food, and water, and a warm place to sleep.

If he couldn't find his family he was going to have to find a way to survive by himself.

He limped slowly down the side of the icy road. Cars would zip by, and each time he did his best to duck out of the way so he wouldn't get hit. None of the cars stopped, or even slowed down. A couple of them beeped their horns at him, and the sound was so loud that he would scramble to safety, his heart pounding wildly.

By the time he got to the centre of town, it was almost dark. Even though there were lots of people around, no one seemed to notice him. One building seemed to be full of good smells, and he trotted around behind it.

There was a tall dustbin back there, and the delicious smells coming from inside it made him so hungry that his stomach hurt. He jumped as high as he could, his claws scrabbling against the rusty metal. He fell far short and landed in a deep pile of snow.

Determined to get some of that food, he picked himself up, shook off the snow and tried again. He still couldn't reach the opening, so he took a running start. This time, he made it a little higher, but he didn't even get close to the top. He fell down into the same drift, panting and frustrated.

The back door of the building opened and a skinny young man about sixteen years old came out. He was wearing a stained white apron and carrying a bulging plastic sack of rubbish. Just as he was about to heave it into the dustbin, he paused.

"Hey!" he said.

The dog was going to run, but he was so hungry that he just stood there and wagged his tail, instead.

"What are you doing here?" the young man asked. Then, he reached out to pat him.

The dog almost bolted, but he made himself stay and let the boy pat him. It felt so good that he wagged his tail even harder.

"Where's your collar?" the boy asked.

The dog just wagged his tail, hoping that he would get patted some more.

"Do you have a name?" the boy asked. "I'm Dominic."

The dog leaned against the boy's leg, still wagging his tail.

Dominic looked him over and then stood up. "*Stay*," he said in a firm voice.

The dog wasn't quite sure what that meant, so he wagged his tail more tentatively. He was very disappointed when he saw the boy turn to go.

Dominic went back inside the building and the door closed after him. He had left the rubbish bag behind and the dog eagerly sniffed it. There was *food* in there. *Lots* of food. He nosed around, looking for an opening, but the bag seemed to be sealed. He nudged at the heavy plastic with an experimental paw, but nothing happened.

He was about to use his teeth when the back door opened again.

Dominic was holding a plate of meatballs and pasta, and glancing back over his shoulder. "Shhh," he said in a low voice as he set the plate down. "My boss'll flip if he sees me doing this."

The dog tore into the meal, gobbling it down so quickly that he practically ate the plastic plate, too. After licking away every last morsel, he wagged his tail at the boy.

"Good dog," Dominic said, and patted him. "Go home now, OK? Your owners must be worried about you."

Patting was *nice*. Patting was very *nice*. Dogs who got to live with people and get patted all the time were *really* lucky. Maybe this boy would take him home. The dog wagged his tail harder, hoping that the boy liked him enough to want to keep him.

"Hey, Dominic!" a voice bellowed. "Get in here! We've got tables to wait on!"

"Be right there!" Dominic called back. He gave the dog one last pat and then stood up.

With one quick heave, he tossed the rubbish bag into the bin. "I have to go. Go home now. Good dog," he said, and went back inside.

The dog watched him leave and slowly lowered his tail. He waited for a while, but the boy didn't come back. He gave the already clean plate a few more licks, waited another few minutes, and then went on his way again.

Oceanport was a small town. Most of the restaurants and shops were clustered together on a few main streets. The town was always quaint, but it looked its best at Christmas time. Brightly coloured lights were strung along the old-fashioned lampposts, and fresh wreaths with red ribbons hung everywhere.

The town square was a beautiful park, where the local orchestra played concerts on the bandstand in the summer. The park also held events like the annual art festival, occasional craft shows and a yearly small carnival. During the holiday season, the various decorations in the park celebrated lots of different cultures and religions. The town council had always described the exhibit of lights and models as "The Festival of Many

Lands". Oceanport was the kind of town that wanted everyone to feel included.

Unfortunately, the dog felt anything *but* included. He wandered sadly through the back alley that ran behind the shops on Main Street. All of the dustbins were too high for him to reach, and the only rubbish bin he managed to tip over was empty. The spaghetti and meatballs had been good, but he was still hungry.

There was water dripping steadily out of a pipe behind a family-owned grocery shop. The drip was too fast to freeze right away and the dog stopped to drink as much of the water as he could. The ice that had formed underneath the drip was very slippery and it was hard to keep his balance. But he managed, licking desperately at the water. Until he started drinking, he hadn't realized how thirsty he really *was*. He licked the water until his stomach was full and he was no longer panting. Then, even though he was alone, he wagged his tail.

Now that he had eaten, and had something to drink, he felt much better. He trotted into the snowy park to look for a place to sleep.

After food, naps were his favourite. The wind was blowing hard, and his short brown fur suddenly felt very thin. He lowered his head and ears as gusts of snow whipped into him.

The most likely shelter in the park was the bandstand and he forced himself through the uneven drifts towards it. The bandstand was an old wooden frame shaped in a circle, with a peaked roof built above it. The steps were buried in snow, and the floor up above them was too exposed to the wind. He could try sleeping on the side facing away from the wind, but that would mean curling up in deep snow. It would be much warmer and more comfortable if he could find a way in underneath it.

The bandstand was set above the ground, with lattice-like boards running around the entire structure. The slats were set fairly far apart and he tried to squeeze between them. Even when he pushed with all of his might, he still couldn't fit. He circled the bandstand several times, looking for a spot where the slats might be broken, but they were in perfect repair.

He was too cold to face lying down in the snow yet, so he decided to keep moving. There was a small white church at the very edge of the park. Its path and steps had been neatly shovelled clear of snow, and when he passed the building, he saw that the front door was ajar.

Heat seemed to be wafting out through the opening and the dog was drawn towards it. Shivering too much to think about being scared, he slipped through the open door.

It was *much* warmer than it had been outside. He gave himself a good, happy shake to get rid of any lingering snow. Then he looked around for a place to rest.

It was a big room, with high, arched ceilings. There were rows of hard wooden benches, separated by a long empty aisle. The church was absolutely silent, and felt very safe. Not sure where to lie down, the dog stood in the centre aisle and looked around curiously. What kind of place was it? Did people *live* here? Would they chase him away, or yell at him? Should he run out now, or just take a chance and hope for the best?

He was so cold and tired that all he wanted to do was lie down. Just as he was about to go and sleep in a back corner, he sniffed the air and then stiffened. There *was* a person in here somewhere! He stood stock-still, his ears up in their full alert position. Instinctively, he lifted one paw, pointing without being sure why he was doing it.

All he knew for certain was that he wasn't alone in here – and he might be in danger!

Chapter 3

He sniffed cautiously and finally located where the scent was. A person was sitting alone in one of the front pews, staring up at the altar. Her shoulders were slouched, and she wasn't moving, or talking. She also didn't seem threatening in any way. In fact, the only thing she seemed to be was unhappy.

The dog hesitated, and then walked up the aisle to investigate. He paused nervously every few steps and sniffed again, but then he would make himself keep going.

It was a young woman in her late twenties, all bundled up in a winter hat, coat and scarf. Her name was Margaret Saunders, and she had lived in Oceanport her whole life. She was sitting absolutely still in the pew, with her hands knotted in her lap. She wasn't making a sound, but there were tears on her cheeks.

The dog stopped at the end of her pew and waved his tail gently back and forth. She seemed very sad, and maybe he could make her feel better.

At first, Margaret didn't see him, and then she flinched.

"You scared me!" she said, with her voice shaking.

The dog wagged his tail harder. She was a nice person; he was *sure* of it.

"You shouldn't be in here," Margaret said sternly.

He cocked his head, still wagging his tail.

"Go on now, before Father Reilly comes out and sees you," she said, and waved him away. "Leave me alone. *Please*." Then she let out a heavy sigh and stared up at the dark altar.

The dog hesitated, and then made his way clumsily into the pew. He wasn't sure how, but maybe he could help her. He rested his head on her knee, and looked up at her with worried brown eyes.

Margaret sighed again. "I thought I said to go away. Where did you come from, anyway? Your owner's probably out looking for you, worried sick."

The dog pushed his muzzle against her folded hands. Automatically, she patted him, and his tail thumped against the side of the pew.

"I hope you're not lost," she said quietly. "It's a bad time of year to feel lost."

The dog put his front paws on the pew. Then, since she didn't seem to mind, he climbed all the way up. He curled into a ball next to her, putting his head on her lap.

"I really don't think you should be up here," she said, but she patted him anyway. She was feeling so lonely that even a scruffy little dog seemed like nice company. She had never had a pet before. In fact, she had never even *wanted* one. Dogs were noisy, and needed to be walked constantly, and shed fur all over the place. As far as she was concerned, they were just more trouble than they were worth. But this dog was so friendly and sweet that she couldn't help liking him.

So they sat there for a while. Sometimes she patted him, and when she didn't, the dog would paw her leg lightly. She would sigh, and then pat him some more. He was getting fur all over her wool coat, but maybe it didn't matter.

"I don't like dogs," she said to him. "Really, I don't. I never have."

The dog thumped his tail.

"*Really*," she insisted, but she put her arm around him. He was pretty cute. If it *was* a he. "Are you a boy dog, or a girl dog?"

The dog just wagged his tail again, looking up at her.

"You know, you have very compassionate eyes," she said, and then shook her head. "What am I, crazy? Talking to a *dog*? As if you're going to *answer* me?" She sighed again. "I don't know, though. I guess I have to talk to *someone*. It's been a long time."

The dog snuggled closer to her. He had never sat like this with a person before, but somehow, it felt very natural. Normal. Almost like cuddling with his brother and sisters.

"My husband died," the woman told him. Then she blinked a few times as her eyes filled with more tears. "We hadn't even been married for two years, and one night –" She stopped and swallowed hard. "He was in a terrible accident," she said finally. "And now – I don't know what to do. It's been almost a year, and – I just feel so alone. And *Christmas* makes it worse." She wiped one hand across her eyes. "We didn't even have time to start a family. And we wanted to have a *big* family."

The dog wanted to make her feel better, but he wasn't sure what to do. He tilted his head, listening intently to words he couldn't understand. Then, for lack of a better idea, he put his paw on her arm. She didn't seem to mind, so he left it there.

"People around here are trying to be really nice to me, especially my parents, but I just can't – I don't know," Margaret said. "I can't handle it. I feel like I can't handle *anything* any more."

The dog cocked his head attentively.

"That's why I only come here at night," she explained, "so I won't have to run into anyone. I used to go to church all the time, but now I don't know how to feel, or what to believe, or – everything's *so hard*. You know?"

The dog watched her with great concentration.

"I can't believe I'm talking to a dog. I must really be losing it." Tentatively, the woman touched his head, and then rubbed his ears. "Is that how I'm supposed to do it? I mean, I've never really patted a dog before."

He wagged his tail.

"What kind of dog are you, anyway?" she asked. "Sort of like one of those police dogs? Except, you're pretty little."

The dog thumped his tail cooperatively.

"Your owners shouldn't let you run around without a collar and licence tag," she said. "They should be more careful."

He lifted his paw towards her, and she laughed. The laugh sounded hesitant, as though she hadn't used it for a very long time.

"OK," she said, and shook his paw. "Why not. Like I told you, I'm not much for dogs, but – that's pretty cute. You seem *smart*."

When she dropped his paw, he lifted it again – and she laughed again.

"Hello?" a voice called from the front of the church. "Is anyone there?"

Now Margaret stiffened. She reached for her purse, getting ready to leave.

Not sure what was wrong, the dog sat up uneasily, too.

An older man wearing black trousers and a black shirt with a white collar came out of a small room near the altar. He was also wearing a thick, handknitted grey cardigan over his shirt. When he saw the woman, he looked surprised.

"I'm sorry, Margaret, I didn't realize you were here," he said. "I was going to lock up for the night."

Margaret nodded, already on her feet. "Excuse me. I was just leaving, Father."

"There's no need for that," he said, and then came part way down the aisle. He paused, leaning against the side of an empty pew. "I haven't seen you for a long time. How have you been?"

Margaret avoided his eyes as she buttoned

her coat and retied her scarf. "Fine, Father Reilly. Everything's just fine. Just – super."

"I saw your parents at eleven o'clock Mass last Sunday," he said conversationally. "They looked well."

Margaret nodded, her head down.

Slowly, Father Reilly let out his breath. "This time of year can be difficult for *anyone*, Margaret. I hope you know that if you ever want to talk, my door is always open."

Margaret started to shake her head, but then she looked down at the dog and hesitated. Maybe it would be nice to talk to someone who could talk *back*. Maybe the dog had been good practice for the real thing.

"I was just going to make myself some tea," Father Reilly said, "if you'd like to come for a few minutes. Maybe we could talk about things, a little. How you're doing."

Margaret looked down at the dog, then back at Father Reilly. She had known Father Reilly since she was a child, and he had always been very sympathetic and under-standing. The kind of priest who was so nice that even people who weren't Catholic would come and talk to him about their problems. "I think I'd like that," she said, her voice hesitant. "Or, anyway, I'd like to try."

"OK, then," Father Reilly said with a kind smile. "It's a place to start, right?" Then his eyebrows went up as he noticed the dog standing in the pew. "Wait a minute. Is that a dog?"

Margaret nodded and patted him again. He wagged his tail in response, but kept his attention on Father Reilly. Was this stranger safe – or someone who was going to chase him away? Would the stranger be nice to his new friend?

"*Your* dog?" Father Reilly asked. "I don't think I've ever seen him around before."

Margaret shook her head. "Oh, no. I really don't even like dogs." Well, maybe she did *now*. A little. "He was just – here."

"Well, maybe we'd better call the police," Father Reilly suggested. "See if anyone has reported him missing. He shouldn't be running around alone in weather like this." He reached his hand out. "Come here, puppy."

Seeing the outstretched hand, the dog

panicked. His mother had taught him that a raised hand usually meant something *bad*. He squirmed out of the pew and bolted down the aisle.

"No, it's OK," Margaret said, hurrying after him. "Come back, dog! You don't have to run away."

The dog stayed uncertainly by the door. Then, as Father Reilly headed down the aisle, too, he made up his mind and raced outside. The winter wind immediately bit into his skin, but he made himself keep running.

The strange man *might* be OK – but he couldn't take that chance.

He ran for what seemed like a long time. When he was exhausted, and quivering from the cold, he finally stopped. He was in an empty car park. There was a long, low red brick building beyond the car park and he followed a shovelled path over to the main entrance. There was some sand on the path, but it didn't hurt his paws the way the road salt had.

The wind was still whipping around and he

ducked his head to avoid it. He couldn't remember *ever* being this cold. Cautiously, he circled the big building until he found a small, sheltered corner. He climbed through a deep drift and then used his front paws to dig some of the snow away.

Once he had cleared away enough snow to make a small nest for himself, he turned around three times and then curled up in a tight ball. The icy temperature of his bed made him shiver, but gradually, his body heat began to fill the space and he felt warmer.

His snow nest wasn't the best bed he had ever had – but, for tonight, it would have to do.

It was going to be another long, lonely night.

Chapter 4

He woke up when he heard children's voices. In fact, there were children *everywhere*. His joints felt frozen, and he had a hard time standing up. He had *never* been cold like this when he slept with his family. He stood there for a minute, in the snow, missing them. In fact, he missed them so much that he didn't even notice how hungry he was. Would he ever find them? Would they ever find *him*?

There were lots of children running around in the snow, yelling and throwing snowballs at each other. Some of them were playing a game with a round red rubber ball, and he *wanted* to bound over and join them.

He ventured out of the sheltered alcove a few steps, then paused. Could he play with them? Would they mind? The game looked like fun.

While he was still making up his mind, the big red ball came rolling in his direction and he barked happily. Then he galloped after it, leaping through the broken snow.

Two boys who were running after the ball stopped when they saw him.

"Where did he come from?" one of the boys, whose name was Gregory Callahan, asked.

The other boy, Oscar Wilson, laughed. "He *looks* like Rudolph!"

Gregory laughed, too. "Oh, so he came from the North Pole?"

"Yep," Oscar said solemnly. "He flew down early. Wanted to beat the holiday traffic."

Gregory laughed again. In a lot of ways, the dog *did* look like Rudolph. Since he was still a puppy, his nose and muzzle were too big for his face. His short fur had the same reddish tint a deer's coat might have, and his legs were very skinny compared to his body. If his nose was red, instead of black, it would be a perfect match.

"Hurry up, you guys!" a girl yelled from the football field. "Break is almost over."

Gregory and Oscar looked at each other, and then chased after the ball.

It was too large to fit in the dog's mouth, so he was pushing it playfully with his paws. Each time the ball veered in a new direction, the dog would lope after it, barking. The whole time, he kept it under control, almost as if he was playing football.

"Check it out," Oscar said, and pushed his glasses up to see better. "We can put him in centre field."

Gregory shook his head, watching the dog chase the ball in circles. "On Charlie Brown's team, maybe. Or, I don't know, the *Cubs*."

Gregory and Oscar were in the fifth grade, and they had been best friends since kindergarten. Although they both loved break more than anything else, Gregory's favourite class was maths, while Oscar liked reading.

Harriet, the girl who had been playing on the wing, ran over to join them. "While you guys were standing here, they scored three goals," she said, with a very critical expression on her face.

Oscar sighed, pretending to be extremely sad. "Downer," he said.

"Big-time," Gregory agreed.

"So go and get the ball," Harriet said.

The boys both shrugged, and watched the dog play.

Harriet put her hands on her hips. "You guys aren't *afraid* of that dumb puppy, are you?"

"Yep," Oscar said, sadly.

Gregory nodded. "*Way* scared."

Harriet was much too caught up in the game to be amused. Instead, she ran after the dog and tried to get the ball away from him.

A game! The dog barked happily and nudged the ball just out of her reach. He would wait until she could almost touch it, and then bat it out of her range again.

Harriet stamped one of her boots in frustration. "Bad dog!" she scolded him. "You bring that ball to me right now!"

The dog barked and promptly knocked the ball further away.

"*That* worked," Gregory said.

"Good effort," Oscar agreed.

Harriet glared at them. "You could *help* me, you know."

Gregory and Oscar thought that over.

"We could," Oscar admitted.

Gregory nodded. "We most definitely could."

"Totally," Oscar said.

But then, of course, they just stayed right where they were and grinned at her. Since she lost her sense of humour pretty easily, Harriet was a lot of fun to tease.

She stamped her foot again. "You're just immature babies! *Both* of you!" Then she ran after the dog as fast as she could.

In the spirit of the game, the dog dodged out of her way. Harriet dived for the ball, missed, and dived again. Then she slipped, landing face-first in a deep mound of snow.

Oscar and Gregory clapped loudly.

"It's not funny," Harriet grumbled as she picked herself up.

Gregory reached behind his back and pre-tended to hold up a large card. "I don't know about you folks judging at home," he said, "but I have to give that one a nine."

Oscar shook his head and held up his own imaginary scoring card. "A seven-point-five is as high as I can go."

"But her compulsories were *beautiful*," Gregory pointed out.

"Well, that's true," Oscar conceded, "but – I'm sorry. The degree of difficulty *just wasn't there*."

"Babies," Harriet said under her breath as she brushed the snow off her down jacket and jeans. "Stupid, immature *babies*."

By now, the rest of the football players had given up on continuing the game and started a wild snowball fight instead. It was so rowdy that at least two teachers had already run over to try and break it up.

Gregory took his gloves off, and then put his fingers in his mouth. It had taken his big sister, Patricia, a long time, but she had finally managed to teach him how to whistle that way. Patricia was convinced that, to have any hope of being cool in life, a person *had* to be able to let out a sharp, traffic-stopping whistle. And, hey, she was in the sixth grade – as far as Gregory was concerned, she *knew* these things.

His hands were a little cold, so his first whistle came out as a wimpy burst of air.

"That's good," Oscar said. "Patty taught you *great*."

Gregory ignored that, and tried again. This time, his whistle was strong and piercing, and half of the kids on the playground looked up from whatever they were doing.

Hearing the sound, the dog froze. His ears went up, and his tail stopped wagging.

"*Stay*," Gregory ordered, and walked over to him.

The dog tilted his head in confusion. Then he gave the ball a tiny, experimental nudge with his nose. Was this part of the game?

"*No*," Gregory said.

The dog stopped.

Gregory patted him on the head. "Good dog," he said. He picked up the ball and tossed it to Harriet.

She caught the ball, and then made a face. "Gross. There's drool all over it."

"Greg can't help it," Oscar said. "He *always* drools. They take him to doctors, but…"

"I almost have it licked," Gregory insisted. "All I have to do is sellotape my mouth shut – and I'm fine."

"*So* immature," Harriet said in disgust, and trotted back to the football field.

A bell rang, signalling the end of break. All over the playground, kids groaned and stopped whatever games they were playing. They headed for the school entrance, where they were supposed to line up in classes before going inside.

"We'd better go, Greg," Oscar said.

Gregory nodded, but he kept patting the dog. His family's collie, Marty, had died recently, and this was the first dog he had patted since then. Marty had been really old – his parents had had him since before he and Patricia were *born* – and life without him was lonely. All of them had cried about it, more than once. His parents had said that they would get another dog sometime soon, but none of them could really face the idea yet, since they still missed Marty so much.

"He doesn't have a collar," Gregory said aloud. "Do you think he's lost?"

Oscar shook his head. "I doubt it. He probably just got out of his garden or something."

Gregory nodded, but he *liked* this dog. If he thought his parents wouldn't get upset, he would bring him home.

Mr Hastings, their teacher, strode over to them. "Come on, boys," he said sternly. "Leave the dog alone. Break is over now."

Gregory would *much* rather have stayed and played with the dog. All afternoon, if possible. But he nodded, and gave the dog one last pat on the head.

"Good dog," he said. "Go home now, boy."

Then he and Oscar followed Mr Hastings towards the school. The dog watched them go, very disappointed. The playground was completely empty now. Slowly, his tail drooped and he lowered his ears. He didn't know why, but for some reason, the game was over.

He was on his own again.

Chapter 5

The dog waited in the playground for a while, but none of the children came back. He was *especially* waiting for the boy who had patted him for so long. He wished that he could *live* with that boy and play with him all the time.

When it was finally obvious that they had gone inside for good, he decided to move on. He walked slowly, with his head down, and his tail between his legs. He was so hungry that his stomach was growling. He ate some snow, but it only made his stomach hurt more.

There were some bins behind the school, overflowing with rubbish bags. Smelling all sorts of wonderful food, he stopped short. He sniffed harder, then started wagging his tail in anticipation. Lunchtime!

The bins were taller than he was, but he climbed on to a pile of snow so he could reach. Then he leaned forward and grabbed one of the bags with his teeth. Using his legs for leverage, he was able to pull the bag free. It fell on to the ground and broke open, spilling half-eaten school lunches everywhere.

It was like a vision of dog heaven. Food, food, and *more* food!

In fact, there was so much food that he really wasn't sure where to start. Lots of sandwich crusts, carrot sticks and apples with one bite out of them. He ate until he was full, switching from leftover peanut butter and jelly to cream cheese and olives to ham. So far, the ham was his favourite. He sniffed the crumpled brown paper bags, hoping to find more.

American cheese, part of a pie, some tuna fish, pudding cartons with some left inside, hard granary rolls, a couple of drumsticks. He ate everything he could find, although he spat all of the lettuce out. He *definitely* didn't like lettuce. Or apples. The rubbish bin smelled more strongly of rotting apples than anything else, although he wasn't sure why.

Some of the milk cartons were still full, and he tore the cardboard containers open. Milk would spurt out on to the snow, and he would quickly lick it up before it drained away. Now his thirst was satisfied, too.

There was so much leftover food that even though he had been starving, he couldn't finish it all. Carefully, he used his front paws to cover the bag with snow. That way, he could come back later and eat some more. And there were other bags he hadn't even opened yet!

He trotted on his way in a much better mood, letting his tail sway jauntily. It didn't even seem as cold any more. He didn't have anywhere special to go, so he decided to wander around town and look for his family. Could they have gone to live with some nice people? Maybe if he went down every street he could find, he would come across them.

The streets were busy with cars full of people doing last-minute holiday shopping.

So, he was very cautious each time he had to cross one. Cars scared him. He would wait by the side of the road until they all seemed to be gone, take a deep breath, and dash across. When he got to the other side, his heart would be beating loudly and he could hear himself panting. No matter how many times he did it, it never got any easier.

He looked and looked, but found no signs that his family had ever existed. He even went back to the old abandoned house to check. The only thing he could find was faint whiffs of his own scent. If they hadn't come back for him by now, he knew they never would.

Tired and discouraged by his long search, it was an effort to keep walking. The sun was going down, and the temperature was dropping again. He wandered morosely through a quiet neighbourhood, looking for a good place to take a nap. When in doubt, he always napped.

He could smell dogs inside some of the warmly lit houses he passed and felt very envious of them. They would bark when he went by, so they must smell him, too. A couple of dogs were outside in fenced yards, and they barked so fiercely at him that he would end up crossing to the other side of the street.

There were tantalizing smells of meat cooking and wood smoke from winter fires wafting out of many of the houses. He would stop on the pavement in front of the best-smelling houses and inhale over and over again. Beef, chicken, pork chops – all *kinds* of good things. He whimpered a little each time he caught a new scent, feeling very sorry for himself.

He was going by a small, unlit white house when he heard a tiny sound. A frail sound. He stopped, his ears flicking up. What was it? A bad sound. A *sad* sound.

He raised his nose into the wind to see if he smelled anything. A person, somewhere nearby. In the snow. He followed his nose – and the low moaning – around to the side of the little house.

There was a car parked in the driveway, and he could still smell petrol and feel the warmth of the engine. Was it going to start up and run over him? He gave the car a wide berth, just in case, but kept tracking the sound.

Suddenly, he saw an old woman crumpled in the snow. She was so limp and still that he had almost stepped on her. There was a sheen of ice on the driveway, and she was lying at the bottom of a flight of steps leading to the back door. Two bags of groceries were strewn haphazardly around her.

She moaned weakly, and he went rigid. He backed away a few steps, and then circled around her a few times. Why didn't she move? When she didn't get up, he let out a small woof.

Her eyes fluttered open and she looked up at him dully. "Help," she whispered. "Please help me."

The dog put a tentative paw on her arm, and she moaned again. He jumped back, afraid. What was wrong? Why was she lying on the ground like that?

Unsure of himself, he ran up the back steps. They were covered with fresh ice and his paws skidded. He barked more loudly, standing up on his hind legs. He scratched at the door with his front paws, still barking.

"No one's there," the old woman gasped. "I live alone."

He barked some more, then ran back down the steps. Why didn't anyone come? Should he bark more?

"*Go*," she said, lifting one arm enough to give him a weak push. "Go and get your owner."

He nosed at her sleeve, and she pushed him harder.

"*Go home*," she ordered, her teeth chattering from the cold. "Get some help!"

The dog didn't know what to do, and he circled her again. There *was* something wrong; he just wasn't sure exactly what it was. Should he curl up with her to keep her warm, or just run away?

At the house across the street, an estate car was pulling into the driveway. He could hear people getting out of the car. There were at least three children, two of whom were bickering.

"Help!" the elderly woman called, but her voice was barely above a whisper. "Help me!"

There was so much urgency in her voice that the dog barked. Then he barked again and again, running back and forth in the driveway. The people noticed him, but still seemed to be going into their house.

He barked more frantically, running part way across the street and then back to the driveway. He repeated the pattern, barking the entire time.

A teenage girl, who was holding a grocery bag and a rucksack full of schoolbooks, laughed. "Whose dog is that?" she asked, pointing over at him. "He's acting like he thinks he's Lassie."

The dog barked loudly, ran up the driveway, and ran out to the street.

"He sure doesn't *look* like Lassie," one of the girl's little brothers, Brett, scoffed. "He looks like a *mutt*."

Their mother, who was carrying her own bags of groceries, frowned. "Maybe something's wrong," she said. "Mrs Amory usually has her lights on by now."

The teenage girl, Lori, shrugged. "Her car's in the driveway. Maybe she's just taking a nap or something."

Her mother still looked worried. "Do me a

favour and go over there, will you, Lori? It can't hurt to check."

Lori shrugged, and gave her grocery bag to Brett and her rucksack to her other brother, Harold.

The dog kept barking and running back and forth as she walked over.

"Take it easy," she said to him. "You've been watching the Discovery Channel or something? Getting *dog ambitions*?"

The dog galloped over to the injured old woman and stood next to her, barking loudly.

Lori's mouth dropped open. "Oh, *whoa*," she said, and then ran over to join him. "Mum!" she yelled over her shoulder. "Call 911! Quick! Mrs Amory's hurt!"

After that, things moved fast. Lori's mother, who was Mrs Goldstein, dashed over to help. Brett went inside to call an ambulance and Harold hurried to get a blanket.

Hearing all the commotion, other neighbours in the area came outside. By the time the police and the ambulance had arrived, a small, concerned crowd had gathered.

Since it was the northwest sector of town,

two of the police officers were Steve and Bill. They worked with the other cops to move the neighbours aside so that the two ambulance attendants could get through with a stretcher.

The whole time, the dog hung back nervously in the shadows of Mrs Amory's garage, not sure if he was in trouble. There were so many people around that he might have done something bad. They all seemed very upset, and it might be his fault.

"What happened, Officer Callahan?" one of the neighbours asked Steve. "Is Mrs Amory going to be OK?"

Steve nodded. "Looks like a broken hip, but the Goldsteins found her in time. She might have a little hypothermia, but she should be just fine."

The ambulance attendants shifted Mrs Amory very gently on to the stretcher, and covered her with two more blankets. She was weak from pain, and shivering from the cold.

"Thank you," she whispered. "Thank you so much."

"Don't worry about a thing," one of the attendants assured her. "We'll have you over at the emergency room in a jiffy."

"He saved me," she said weakly. "I don't know where he came from, but he saved me."

"Well, don't worry, you're going to be fine," the attendant said comfortingly.

As she was lifted into the back of the ambulance, Steve and Bill and the other officers moved the onlookers aside.

"Let's clear away now," Bill said authoritatively. "Give them room to pull out."

The ambulance backed slowly out of the driveway, with its lights flashing and its siren beginning to wail. Everyone watched as the emergency vehicle drove away with Mrs Amory safely inside.

"OK, folks, show's over," Steve announced. "Thanks a lot for all of your help. You can head in for supper now."

Although there was still an eager buzz of conversation, most of the neighbours started drifting towards their houses.

Bill pulled out his notebook and went over to the Goldsteins. "We just need a few things for our report," he said to Mrs Goldstein. "You and your daughter found her?"

"It was Lassie!" Lori's little brother Harold chirped. "He was totally cool!"

Bill looked sceptical. "What do you mean by that, son?"

Brett pointed at the dog crouching by the garage. "It was that dog!" he said, sounding just as excited as Harold. "He was barking and barking, and Lori followed him. It was just like TV!"

Bill's expression became even more doubtful. "You're saying that a *dog* came over to get help?"

"Exactly," Mrs Goldstein answered for her sons. "I know it must sound strange – but he was very insistent, and that's when I sent Lori over. I was afraid that something might be wrong."

Bill digested that, his pen still poised over the empty notebook page. "So, wait, let me get this straight. It was *your* dog who alerted you?" he asked.

"We don't have a dog," Brett told him.

Harold nodded, looking sheepish. "On account of, I'm allergic," he said, and sniffed a little to prove it.

Bill considered all of that, and then squinted over towards the garage. "You sure the dog didn't knock her down in the first place?"

"I don't think so," Lori said doubtfully. "He was trying to help."

It was completely dark now, except for the headlights on the two remaining squad cars. Bill unclipped his torch from his equipment belt. He turned it on and flashed the light around the yard.

Seeing it, the dog instinctively shied away from the beam. But it was too late – Bill had already seen him.

"Hey!" Bill said, and nudged his partner. "It's that same stray dog you were so hot about catching the other night."

"What about him?" Steve asked, in the middle of taking a statement from one of the other neighbours.

"He's over there," Bill said, and gestured with the torch. "The Goldsteins say he sounded the alarm."

Steve's eyebrows went up. "Really? Hey, all right! I *told* you he was a great dog." He shoved his notebook in his jacket pocket. "Let's see if we can get him this time. Find him a good home."

All of the neighbours wanted to help capture the hero dog. So everyone fanned out and moved forward. Some of them shouted, "Here, boy!" while others whistled or snapped their fingers.

Seeing so many people coming towards him, the dog slipped deeper into the bushes. He *was* in trouble! They had taken the poor old lady away, and now they were *blaming* him. He squirmed towards the woods crouched down on all fours, trying to stay out of sight. Then, he gathered all of his energy and started running as fast as he could.

Lately, escaping to safety had become one of his best tricks!

Chapter 6

The dog hid in the woods until he was *sure* that no one was coming after him any more. It had been a very long day, and all he wanted to do now was *sleep*. He could walk back to the school and sleep in that little alcove, but it seemed too far.

There was a pile of boulders to his right and he crept over to explore them. Most of the rocks were jammed close together and buried in snow. But a few had openings that looked like little caves. He chose the one that seemed to be the most private and wiggled inside.

He fitted easily, and there was even room to stand up and turn around, if he wanted.

Almost no snow had blown in, and there were lots of dry leaves to lie on. He could smell the musty, ancient odour of other animals who had used this cave for a shelter – squirrels, mostly, and maybe a skunk or two. But, as far as he could tell, no other animal had been in here for a long time.

As always, he turned around three times before lying down. The cave was so warm, compared to being outside, that he slept for a long time.

When he woke up and poked his head out through the rock opening, it was snowing hard. He retreated back inside. He wanted to go over to the school and find some more discarded lunches to eat, but the storm was just too bad. No matter how much his stomach started growling, he would be much better off in here, out of the blizzard. The wind was howling, and he was glad to be in a place where he could avoid it.

So, he went back to sleep. Every so often, he would be startled by a noise and leap to his feet. Then, when it turned out to be nothing out of the ordinary, he would curl up again.

It snowed all day, and most of the night. He only went outside to go to the toilet, and then he would return to his little rock cave. The snow was so deep now that his legs were completely buried when he tried to walk, and mostly he had to leap. Leaping was hard work, and made him tired after a while. He liked it better when there wasn't any snow at all. Grass and dirt were *easy* to walk on.

Once, he saw a chipmunk chattering away on a low tree branch. He was hungry, and thought about trying to catch the little animal. But before he could even *try* to lunge in that direction, the chipmunk had sensed danger and scampered further up the tree. He ducked back into his cave, not terribly disappointed. The poor little chipmunk was trying to survive the harsh winter, the same way he was. He would just go hungry today, that's all.

By the next morning, the storm had finally stopped. The temperature was higher than it had been, and the top layer of snow was already softening into slush.

He hadn't eaten for such a long time that he headed straight for the school rubbish bins.

When he got to the school, he stopped in the car park and shook out each front paw, since he had snow caked between his toes. Now, it was time to eat some breakfast.

He ran around behind the building, but the rubbish bins were empty! Now what? He had been so sure that he would find more ham, pies, and other treats.

He sank back on to his haunches and whimpered a couple of times. Where had all the food gone? The rubbish bins were closed now and piled high with snow. All he could smell was the lingering stench of rotten apples and sour milk. They weren't very nice smells, but his stomach still rumbled.

He prowled around the back of the school for a while. Then he came to a door where he could smell food. He barked a couple of times, then sat down to see what would happen. The *last* time he had smelled food behind a door, that teenage boy had given him those great meatballs. Maybe he would get lucky again.

The door opened and a very stout woman in a big white apron looked out. She was Mrs Gustave, the school cook.

"What?" she asked in a loud, raspy voice.

The dog barked again and held up one paw.

"Hmmm," Mrs Gustave said, and folded her arms across her huge stomach. "Is that the best you can do?"

She seemed to be waiting for something, so he sat back and lifted both paws in the air.

"That's better," she decided, and disappeared into the kitchen.

Even though she was gone, the dog stayed in the same position. Maybe if she came back, she would like it more the second time. Then he lost his balance and fell over on his side.

"*My* dog can do much better than that," Mrs Gustave said. She had come outside just in time to see him tumble into the snow.

He quickly scrambled up and held out one paw. One paw was *definitely* safer than two.

"You're going to have to work on that," she said. With a grunt of effort, she bent over and set a steaming plate on top of the snow.

It was crumbled hamburger with gravy, served over mashed potatoes. He wagged his tail enthusiastically and started eating.

"Now, remember," Mrs Gustave said.

"From now on, you should eat at *home* and not go around begging like a fool." Then she closed the door so she could go back to cooking the students' hot lunch.

He enjoyed his meal very much, and licked the plate over and over when he was done. It had been a hefty serving, but he still could have eaten five or six more. Still, the one big portion made him feel much better.

Cheerfully, he wandered around to the playground. Maybe his friends from the other day would come out again! Then he might get patted some more.

He waited for a long time, and then he got bored. He scratched a little, dug a couple of holes in the snow, and then rolled over a few times.

But he was still bored. He yawned, and scratched again. Still bored. It was time for a nap.

He trudged over to the sheltered area where he had slept that one night. He dug himself a new nest, stamping down the snow with all four feet. Then he lay down and went right to sleep. He slept very soundly, and even snored a little. The day passed swiftly.

"Hey, look!" a voice said. "He *did* come back!"

The dog opened his eyes to see Gregory and his friend Oscar standing above him. He wagged his tail and sprang to his feet.

"Where've you been?" Gregory asked, patting him. "We looked all over for you yesterday."

The dog wagged his tail harder and let them take turns patting him.

"You know, he's kind of scraggly," Oscar said. "Maybe he really *is* a stray."

Gregory shrugged. "Of course he is. Why else would he sleep here?"

Oscar bent down and sniffed slightly. Then he made a face and straightened up. "I think he needs a *bath*, too."

Gregory thought about that. "My father's always home writing, so I can't sneak him into my house. What about your house?"

Oscar shook his head. "Not today. Delia and Todd have the flu, so Mum had to stay home with them."

The dog tried to sit up with both paws in

the air again, but fell over this time, too.

Both boys laughed.

"What a goofball," Oscar said.

Gregory nodded. "He's funny, though. I really like him."

"Why don't you just say you want a dog for Christmas?" Oscar suggested. "Then you can show up with him like it's a big surprise."

Gregory was very tempted by that idea, but he was pretty sure it wouldn't work. "I don't know," he said doubtfully. "My parents said we could maybe go and pick one out together in a month or two."

Oscar packed together a hard snowball and flipped it idly from one hand to the other. "What does Patricia say?" he asked.

Gregory's big sister. Her advice was advice Gregory always took seriously. Gregory sighed. "That they're still much too sad to even *look* at other dogs right now."

Oscar nodded, then threw the snowball a few feet away. The dog promptly chased after it, and brought it back.

Gregory looked pleased. "He fetches! He's really smart!"

Oscar laughed and threw the snowball even further. "How smart is a dog who fetches *snow?*" he asked as the dog returned with the snowball, his tail beating wildly from side to side.

"*Extra*-smart," Gregory said.

Oscar shrugged and tossed the snowball twenty feet away. "If you say so."

The dog galloped happily after it.

"Boys!" a sharp voice yelled. "What are you doing over there?" It was Ms Hennessey, one of their teachers. She was always *very* strict.

Gregory and Oscar looked guilty, even though they weren't really doing anything wrong at all.

"Science," Oscar said. "We were just standing here, talking a whole lot about science."

Gregory nodded. "Like, gravity and stuff." He made his own snowball and flicked it straight up into the air.

They both watched it come down, shook their heads, and exchanged admiring glances.

"Gravity again," Oscar observed solemnly. "*Cool.*"

The dog picked up that snowball instead

and offered it to Gregory.

Ms Hennessey marched over, her face tight with concern. She was tall and extremely skinny, with lots of bright red hair. She liked to wear wide, billowy skirts, big sunglasses and ponchos. "Don't you boys know better than to go up to a stray animal! It's *dangerous*!"

This little dog might be many things, but "dangerous" didn't seem to be one of them. Gregory and Oscar looked at each other, and shrugged.

"Get away from him right now!" Ms Hennessey said with her hands on her hips. "He might have rabies!"

Gregory looked at the dog, who wagged his tail in a very charming way. "I don't think so, ma'am. He seems –"

"Look at him!" Ms Hennessey interrupted, and pulled both of the boys away. "There's *foam* in his mouth!"

"That's just drool, ma'am," Oscar explained. "Because he's sort of panting."

Gregory gave him a small shove. "Saliva, Oscar. Us science types like to call it saliva."

"Well, I'm going to call the dog officer," Ms

Hennessey said grimly. "We can't have a dangerous dog roaming around near children. I just won't have it!"

For years, Gregory's parents had always explained to him that it was important to be *careful* around strange animals – but that it was *also* important to help any animal who might be in trouble. "Please don't call the dog officer, Ms Hennessey," he said desperately. If the dog went to the pound, he would never get to see him again. "It's OK, he's –" Gregory tried to come up with a good excuse – "he's *my* dog! He just – followed me to school, that's all."

Ms Hennessey narrowed her eyes. "Where's his collar?"

Gregory thought fast. "He lost it, when we were walking on the beach last weekend."

"A seagull probably took it," Oscar put in helpfully. "They like shiny things."

"*Racoons* like shiny objects," Gregory told him. "Not seagulls."

"Oh." Oscar shrugged. "That's right, it was a racoon. I heard it was a big old *family* of racoons."

Ms Hennessey wasn't buying any of this. "What's his name?" she asked.

Gregory and Oscar looked at each other.

"Sparky," Gregory said, just as Oscar said, "Rover."

Ms Hennessey nodded, her suspicions confirmed. "I see."

"His, um, his *other* nickname is Spot," Gregory said, rather lamely.

"I don't appreciate having you two tell me fibs," Ms Hennessey said without a hint of a smile on her face. "I think you'd just better come along down to the office with me, and you can talk to Dr Garcia about all of this."

Dr Garcia was the vice principal – and she made Ms Hennessey seem *laid-back*. Being sent to the office at Oceanport Middle School was always a major disaster, dreaded by one and all.

"But –" Gregory started to protest.

"Come along now," Ms Hennessey ordered, taking each of them by the sleeve. She turned towards Ms Keise, one of the other teachers. "Cheryl, chase this dog away from here! He's a threat to the children!"

"He's not," Gregory insisted. "He's a really *good* –"

"That will be quite enough of that," Ms Hennessey said sharply, and led the two of them away.

The dog let the snowball fall out of his mouth. Where were his friends going? Then he saw a tall woman in a leather coat hurrying towards him. She was frowning and shaking her finger at him. Before the woman could get any closer, the dog started running.

He would much rather run away – than be *chased*.

Chapter 7

The dog ended up hiding behind the rubbish bins. When he no longer heard any voices, he slogged back to his little alcove to sleep some more. Who knew when his friends might come back? He wanted to be here waiting when they did.

This time, though, the voice that woke him up was female. He opened one eye and saw a thin girl, with her hair tied back in a neat brown ponytail. She had the same very blue eyes Gregory had, and she was wearing a red, white and blue New England Patriots jacket. It was Patricia, Gregory's big sister.

"So, you must be the dog my brother won't shut up about," she said aloud.

The dog cocked his head.

Patricia frowned at him. "He got *detention* because of you. So even though it's Christmas, Mum and Dad are probably going to have to ground him."

He wagged his tail tentatively. She didn't exactly sound mad, but she didn't sound friendly, either.

"Well," she said, and tossed her ponytail back. "The way he was going on and on, I figured you could *talk* or something. Tap dance and sing, maybe. But you just look normal. Even a little silly, if you want to know the truth."

Maybe she would like it if he rolled in the snow. Like *him*. So, he rolled over a couple of times.

"*A lot* silly," she corrected herself.

The dog scrambled up and shook vigorously. Snow sprayed out in all directions.

"Thanks a lot, dog," Patricia said, and wiped the soggy flakes from her face and jacket. "I enjoyed that."

He wagged his tail.

"We could still maybe talk Mum and Dad

into it. I mean, it *is* almost Christmas," she said. "Although we really like *collies*." She studied him carefully. "It would be easier if you had a limp, or your ear was chewed up, or something. Then my parents would feel sorry for you."

The dog barked. Then he sat down and held up his right paw.

Patricia nodded. "Not bad. If you could *walk* with your paw up like that, they could *never* say no. Here, try it." She clapped her hands to be sure she had his full attention. "*Come*."

Obediently, the dog walked over to her. "Come" was an easy one.

"No, *limp*," she said, and demonstrated. "I want you to limp. Like this, see?" She hopped around on one red cowboy-booted foot. Cowboy boots might not be warm in the winter, but they *were* cool. Always. "Can you do that?"

The dog barked, and rolled over in the snow. Then he bounded to his feet and looked at her hopefully.

"Well, that's not right at all," she said, and

76

then sighed. "If I tell you to play dead, you'll probably *sit*, right?" She shook her head in dismay. "I really don't know about this. I thought he said you were smart."

The dog barked and wagged his tail heartily.

"Right," Patricia said, and shook her head again. "And if I tell you to 'Speak', you're going to look for a hoop to jump through – I can see it now."

Perplexed by all of this, the dog just sat down and looked at her blankly.

"Well, this is just a waste," Patricia said, and then straightened the tilt of her beret. "Until we can get you home and I have some serious training time with you, you're clearly *beyond* my help." She unzipped her rucksack and took out some crackers and cheese and two chicken sandwiches. "Here, we saved most of our lunches for you. The crackers are from Oscar." She placed the food down in the snow. "Don't ever say I didn't do anything for you."

The dog wagged his tail, and then gobbled up the food in several gulping bites.

"We'll bring more tomorrow, even though it's Saturday," Patricia promised. "Greg can't come back this afternoon because Dad's going to have to pick him up after detention and yell at him for a while. You know, for appearances."

The dog licked the napkin for any remaining crumbs. Then he stuck his nose underneath it, just in case. But he had polished off every last scrap.

"See you later then," she said, and jabbed her finger at him. "Stay. OK? *Stay*."

The dog lifted his paw.

"Ridiculous," Patricia said, and walked away, shaking her head the entire time. "Just ridiculous."

The dog hung around the school until all the lights were out, and even the janitors had gone home. Then he decided to roam around town for a while. He took what had become his regular route, heading first to the abandoned house. There was no sign of his family – which didn't surprise him, but *did* disappoint him.

Again.

After that, he wandered through the various neighbourhoods, looking longingly at all of the families inside their houses. He explored the back alleys behind Main Street. The drainpipe near the pizza place was still leaking, and he had a nice, long drink.

Visiting the park was the next stop on his route. There were lots of townspeople strolling down the winding paths and admiring the holiday exhibits. He was careful to stay out of sight, but he enjoyed being around all of the activity. It was almost like being *part* of it.

There was a traditional Nativity scene, complete with a manger and plastic models of barnyard animals and the Three Wise Men. Further along, there were displays honouring Chanukah, Kwanzaa, and various other ways of celebrating the holiday season.

There was also, of course, a big, wooden sleigh. A fat model Santa Claus sat inside it, surrounded by presents, and the sleigh was being pulled by eight tiny plastic reindeer. Coloured lights decorated all of the trees, and the little model of Main Street had been built perfectly to scale, right down to the miniature people cluttering its pavements.

Christmas carols and other traditional songs played from the loudspeaker above the bandstand, every night from six to ten. On Christmas Eve, live carollers would gather there and hold an early evening concert for everyone to enjoy. Oceanport took the holiday season *seriously*.

He found a nice vantage point underneath a mulberry bush, and settled down for a short nap. When he opened his eyes, the park had cleared out and all of the holiday lights had been turned off for the night. The place *seemed* to be deserted.

He wasn't sure what had woken him up, but somewhere, he heard a suspicious noise. Laughter. Low male voices. Banging and crunching sounds. He stood up, the fur slowly rising on his back. Something wasn't right. He should go and investigate the situation.

The voices were coming from over near the crèche. The dog loped silently through the snow, approaching the Nativity scene from behind. The laughter was louder and he could hear people hissing "Shhh!" to one another.

Whatever they were doing, it didn't feel right. There was a crash, and then more laughter. The dog walked around to the front of the crèche, growling low in his throat.

Inside the Nativity scene, a group of boys from the high school were moving the plastic figures around. They had always been bullies, and vandalism was one of their favourite destructive pranks. They were especially active during the holidays.

One of them was just bending down to steal the baby Jesus figure from the manger. Two other boys were walking over to the Chanukah exhibit, holding cans of spray paint. The fourth boy was knocking over the Three Wise Men, one at a time.

The dog growled the most threatening growl he knew how to make, and all of the boys froze.

"Whose dog?" one of them, Luke, asked uneasily.

The other three shrugged.

"Dunno," the biggest one, Guillermo, said. "Never seen him before."

The dog growled and took a stiff-legged step forward.

"Hey, *chill*, dog!" Michael, the leader of the group, said impatiently. "We're only fooling around." He turned to his friends. "Ignore him – it's just a dumb puppy. Let's hurry up before someone sees us."

"Hey, he looks kind of like those reindeer," another boy, Rich, said, sniggering. "Let's tie him up front there."

Luke held up his can of red spray paint. "If you guys hold him, I'll spray his nose!"

They all laughed.

"Let's do it!" Michael decided.

As they crept towards him, the dog growled, his lips curling away from his teeth.

"Oh, yeah," Guillermo said. "He thinks he's *tough*."

"Let's leave *him* in the manger," Rich suggested. "That'd be pretty funny!"

As Luke and Michael lunged for him, the dog snarled and leaped forward. With his teeth bared, he slashed at Michael's jacket.

The sleeve tore, and Michael stopped short. He looked down at the jagged rip and started swearing.

"That's *Gore-Tex*, man," he protested. "You stupid dog!" He aimed a kick at the dog's head, but missed. "It was really expensive! How'm I going to *explain* this?" He tried another kick, but the dog darted out of the way.

Guillermo packed together a ball of ice and snow. Then he threw it as hard as he could. The chunk hit the dog square in the ribs and he yelped.

"Yeah, all right!" Guillermo shouted, and bent down to find some more ice. "Let's get 'im!"

The dog growled at them, and then started barking as loudly as he could. He barked over and over, the sound echoing through the still night.

"If he doesn't shut up, everyone in town's going to hear him," Luke said uneasily.

"We mess up these dumb exhibits *every* year," Rich complained. "We can't let some stupid dog ruin this – it's a *tradition*."

During all of the commotion, none of them had noticed the police squad car patrolling past the park. The car stopped and Officers Kathy Bronkowski and Tommy Lee got out. They had been two of the other cops at Mrs Amory's house the night before, when she had broken her hip on the ice.

Officer Lee turned on his torch, while Officer Bronkowski reached for her nightstick. When the beam passed over them, the boys were exposed in the bright light and they all stood stock-still for a few seconds.

"Hey!" Officer Bronkowski yelled. "What do you think you're doing over there!"

The boys started running, stumbling over one another in their hurry to get away.

"Get back here, you punks!" Officer Lee shouted. "You think we don't recognize you?"

Still furious, the dog raced after them. He snapped at their heels, just to scare them a little. It *worked*. He kept chasing them all the way to the end of the park. Then he trotted back to the crèche, barely panting at all.

The two police officers were carefully reassembling the exhibit. They brushed snow off the tipped-over figures, and then set each one in its proper place.

Officer Bronkowski picked up the two discarded cans of spray paint. "Those little creeps," she said under her breath. "Who do they think they are?"

Officer Lee put the baby Jesus figure gently in the manger. "I saw Michael Smith and Guillermo Jereda. Did you get a good look at the other two?"

Officer Bronkowski shook her head. She had long blonde hair, but when she was on duty, she kept it pinned up in a bun. "No, but it was probably the Crandall twins, Luke and Rich. Those four are always together."

"So let's cruise by their houses," Officer Lee suggested. "See what their parents have to say about this."

Officer Bronkowski nodded. "Good idea. It's about time we caught them in the act."

"The dog gave them away," Officer Lee said, with a shrug. He yawned, opened a pack of gum, and offered a piece to his partner before taking one for himself. "They shouldn't have brought him along."

Officer Bronkowski started to answer, but then she noticed the dog lurking around behind the scale model of the Oceanport town hall. "You know what? I don't think they did," she said slowly.

Officer Lee glanced up from the plastic donkey he was setting upright. "What do you mean?"

She pointed at the dog. "Unless I'm crazy, that's the same dog who found Mrs Amory yesterday."

Officer Lee looked dubious. "Oh, come on. You mean you think there's some dog *patrolling* Oceanport? You're starting to sound like Steve Callahan." Steve Callahan was, of course, the police officer who had been trying to catch the dog ever since he saw him at the abandoned house. Steve Callahan was also, as it happened, Gregory and Patricia's uncle.

Officer Bronkowski nodded. "That's exactly what I'm saying. Would we have pulled over just now if we hadn't heard him barking?"

"Well, no," Officer Lee admitted, "but—"

Officer Bronkowski cut him off. "And if Gail Amory had been out much longer last night, the doctors say she might have frozen to death. She owes her *life* to that dog."

Officer Lee grinned at her. "So let's put him on the payroll. Maybe even arrange a Christmas bonus." He gave the dog a big thumbs-up. "Good dog! Way to go!"

The dog barked once, and then trotted off.

"Wait!" Officer Bronkowski called after him. "Come back!"

The dog kept going. It was time to be on his way again.

Chapter 8

Remembering how warm it had been inside, the dog went back to the church. Unfortunately, tonight, the door was firmly closed. He leaned his shoulder against it and pushed, but the heavy wood wouldn't even budge.

OK. New plan. He would go back to the school, maybe. In the morning, his friends might come back. Gregory, especially, although he liked Oscar and Patricia, too. Maybe they would even have more food for him! Those chicken sandwiches were *good*.

He was cutting across a car park, when he heard – crying. A child, crying. It might even be a baby. He stopped to listen, lifting his paw. The sound was coming from a car parked at the farthest end of the car park.

He ran right over, stopping every few feet to sniff the air. There were several people in the car – he could smell them – but the crying was coming from a small child. A small, miserable child. A sick child.

All of the car windows were rolled up, except for the one on the driver's side, which was cracked slightly. The car was a beat-up old estate car, and it was *crammed* with people and possessions. He could hear a soothing female voice trying to calm the crying child. The baby would cry, and then cough, and then cry some more. There were two other children in the back seat, and he could hear them coughing and sneezing, too.

He barked one little bark.

Instantly, everyone inside the car, except for the baby, was silent. They were maybe even holding their breaths.

He barked again.

One of the doors opened partway, and a tow-headed little boy peeked out.

"Mummy, it's a dog!" he said. "Can we let

him in?"

"No," his mother answered, sounding very tired. "Close the door, Ned. It's cold out there."

"*Please?*" Ned asked. "He won't eat much – I promise! He can have my share."

His mother, Jane Yates, just sighed. They had been homeless since the first of the month, and she could barely afford to feed her *children*. She, personally, had been living on one tiny meal a day for almost two weeks now. For a while, after the divorce, she had been able to keep things going fine. But then, her ex-husband left the state and right after Thanksgiving, she got laid off. Since then, their lives had been a nightmare. And now, all three of the children were sick with colds. The baby, Sabrina, was running a fever, and her cough was so bad that she was probably coming down with bronchitis. They didn't have any money to pay a doctor, so the baby was just getting sicker and sicker.

"I'm sorry, Ned," Jane said. "We just can't. I'm really sorry."

Now Ned started crying, too. His sister,

Brenda, joined in – and the baby, Sabrina, had yet to stop.

"Go away," Jane said to the dog, sounding pretty close to tears herself. "Please just leave us alone." She reached over the front seat and yanked the back door closed.

The door slammed in the dog's face and he jumped away, startled. Now *all* he could hear was crying and coughing. What was going on here? It was bad, whatever it was.

He pawed insistently at the door, and barked again. No matter what he did, the crying wouldn't stop.

"Bad dog! Go away!" Jane shouted from inside the car. "Stop bothering us!"

The dog backed off, his ears flattening down against his head. He circled the car a couple of times, but none of the doors opened. These people needed help! With one final bark, he trotted uncertainly back towards the church.

When he got there, Margaret Saunders, the young widow he had met earlier that week, was just coming out with her mother. If they didn't exactly look overjoyed, at least they seemed to be at peace.

"Well, hi there," Margaret said, her face lighting up when she saw him. She reached down one gloved hand to pat him. "Mum, it's the dog I was telling you about. He's pretty cute, isn't he?"

Her mother nodded.

"Maybe I should *get* a dog, sometime," Margaret mused. "To keep me company."

"Sounds like a great idea," her mother agreed. Since Saunders had been Margaret's husband's last name, her mother was Mrs Talbot.

Margaret patted the dog again. "I think so, too. Whoever owns *this* dog is pretty lucky."

"No doubt. But I can't help wondering if maybe someone *sent* him to you that night," her mother said softly, and smiled at her daughter.

Margaret smiled back. Her mother had a point. The dog *had* appeared out of nowhere. "Stranger things have happened, I guess."

Margaret might be patting his head, but otherwise, they didn't seem to be paying much attention to him. He could still, faintly, hear the sound of crying, and he barked loudly. One thing the dog had learned, was that if he barked a lot, he could get people to follow him. He just *knew* that baby shouldn't be crying like that. He dashed off a few steps, barked, and ran back to them.

Margaret grinned. She had been feeling a little happier over the last couple of days. Hopeful, for the first time in many months. "What do you think, Mum? *I* think he's telling us that Timmy fell down the mine shaft, and we're supposed to bring rope."

Her mother laughed. "It certainly looks that way." Of course, neither of them was used to dogs. But *this* one seemed to have come straight out of a movie.

The dog barked again, and ran a few steps away. He barked more urgently, trying to make them understand.

Father Reilly came outside to see what all the commotion was. "What's going on?" he asked, buttoning his cardigan to block out some of the wind.

"Look, Father," Margaret said, and gestured towards the street. "That nice dog is back."

Father Reilly nodded, and then shivered a

little. "So he is. But – what's wrong with him?"

The dog barked, and ran away three more steps.

"I don't know," Margaret's mother answered. "I don't know much about animals, but he really seems to want us to follow him."

Father Reilly shrugged. "Well, he strikes me as a pretty smart dog. Let's do it."

So, with that, they all followed him. The dog led them straight to the car park. He checked over his shoulder every so often to make sure that they were still behind him. If he got too far ahead, he would stop and wait. Then, when they caught up, he would set forth again.

He stopped right next to the sagging estate car and barked. The baby was still coughing and wailing.

The driver's door flew open and Jane Yates got out.

"I told you to go away!" she shouted, clearly at the end of her tether.

Father Reilly stared at her. "Jane, is that you? What are you doing here?"

Realizing that the dog was no longer alone, Jane blushed. "Oh," she said, and avoided their eyes. She hadn't expected company. "Hi." Sabrina coughed and she automatically picked her up, wrapping a tattered blanket more tightly around her so she would be warm.

"You have the children in there with you?" Margaret's mother asked, sounding horrified.

"I couldn't help it," Jane said defensively. "We didn't have any other place to go. Not that it's anyone else's business. Besides, they're *fine*. We're all fine."

Since it was obvious to everyone that the family *wasn't* fine, nobody responded to that. Sometimes it was easy to forget that even in nice, small towns like Oceanport, people could still be homeless.

"Why didn't you come to the church?" Father Reilly asked. "Or the shelter? We would have helped you."

Jane scuffed a well-worn rubber boot against the snow. "I was too embarrassed," she muttered.

Again, no one knew what to say. The baby sneezed noisily, and clung to her mother.

Father Reilly broke the silence. "Still, you must know that you could *always* come to the church," he said. "No matter what."

"I'm not even *Catholic*," Jane reminded him.

Ned, and his sister Brenda, had climbed out of the car and were patting the dog. They got him to sit in the snow, and took turns shaking hands with him. Each time, they would laugh and the dog would wag his tail. Then, they would start the game all over again.

"It's not about religion, it's about community," Father Reilly answered. "About *neighbours*."

Jane's shoulders were slumped, but she nodded.

"Look," Margaret's mother said, sounding very matter-of-fact. "The important thing here is to get these poor children in out of the cold. And the baby needs to see a doctor, right away."

"I don't have any—" Jane started.

"We'll take her to the emergency room," Mrs Talbot said. "Before she gets pneumonia."

Father Reilly checked his watch. "We won't be able to get into the shelter tonight, but after that, why don't I take you over to the convent and see if the sisters can put you up for the night. Then, tomorrow, we can come up with a better plan."

Jane hesitated, even though her teeth were chattering. "I'm not sure. I mean, I'd rather—"

"You have to do *something*," Margaret's mother said. "Once you're all inside, and get a hot meal, you'll be able to think more clearly."

"Come on," Father Reilly said. "I'll drive everyone in my car."

Throughout all of this, Margaret stayed quiet. Although Jane had been two years ahead of her, they had actually gone to high school together. Since then, their lives had moved in very different – if equally difficult – directions. It wouldn't have seemed possible that things could turn out this way, all those years ago, playing together on the softball team. The team had even been undefeated that year. In those days, they *all* felt un-defeated. She shook her head and stuffed her hands into her pockets. Little had they known back then how easily – and quickly – things could go wrong.

Now, Jane looked at her for the first time. "Margaret, I, uh, I was really sorry to hear about what happened. I know I should have written you a note, but – I'm sorry."

Margaret nodded. When a person's husband was killed suddenly, it was hard for other people to know how to react. What to say, or do. "I guess we've both had some bad luck," she answered.

Jane managed a weak smile, and hefted Sabrina in her arms. "Looks that way, yeah."

They both nodded.

"So it's settled," Father Reilly said. "We'll lock up here, and then I'll run you all over to the hospital, and we can go to the convent from there."

Margaret's mother nodded. "Yes. I think that's the best plan, under the circumstances."

Seeing the shame and discomfort on Jane's face, Margaret felt sad. Then she thought of something. "I – I have an idea," she ventured.

They all looked at her.

Margaret turned to direct her remarks to Jane. "Dennis and I bought a big house, because –" Because they had wanted to have a *big* family. "Well, we just did," she said, and had to blink hard. "Anyway, I –" She stopped, suddenly feeling shy. "I have *lots* of room, and maybe – for a while, we could – I don't know. I'd like it if you came to stay with me, until you can get back on your feet again. What do you think?"

Jane looked shy, too. "We couldn't impose like that. It wouldn't be –"

"It *would* be," Margaret said with great confidence. "I think it would be *just* the right thing – for both of us." She bent down to smile at Ned and Brenda. "What do you think? Do you all want to come home with me and help me – deck my halls?" This would give her a reason to buy a Christmas tree. Even to celebrate a little.

"Can we, Mum?" Brenda pleaded.

Jane hesitated.

"I think it's a wonderful idea," Father Reilly said, and Margaret's mother nodded.

"Please," Margaret said quietly. "You may not believe this, but it would probably help *me* out, more than it's going to help you."

Jane grinned wryly and gestured towards the possessions-stuffed car. "You're right," she agreed. "I don't believe it."

Margaret grinned, too. "But you'll come?"

"If you'll have us," Jane said, looking shy.

"Actually, I think it's going to be great," Margaret said.

Standing alone, off to the side, the dog wagged his tail. Everyone seemed happy now. Even the baby wasn't really crying any more, although she was still coughing and sneezing. He could go somewhere and get some much-needed sleep. In fact, he was *long* overdue for a nap.

"Can we bring the dog with us, too, Mummy?" Ned asked. "Please?"

"Well –" Jane glanced at Margaret, who nodded. "Sure. I think we should."

They all looked around to see where the dog was.

Margaret frowned as she scanned the empty car park. The dog was nowhere in sight. "That's funny," she said. "I'm sure he was here just a minute ago."

They all called and whistled, but there was no response.

The dog was gone.

Chapter 9

Walking along the dark streets, the dog was just plain exhausted. The park was much closer than the school, so he went there to find a place to sleep. He was going to go back underneath his mulberry bush, but it was a little bit too windy. So he took a couple of minutes to scout out another place instead.

There was lots of straw piled up in the Nativity scene, but it felt scratchy against his skin. None of the other models were big enough for him to squeeze inside. He was about to give up and go under the bush, when he saw the sleigh. It was stuffed tight with the Santa model and the make-believe gifts, but maybe there would be room for him, too.

Wool blankets were piled around the gifts to make it look as though they were spilling out of large sacks. He took a running start, and leaped right into Santa's lap. Then he squirmed out of sight underneath the blankets. The blankets were almost as scratchy as the hay had been, but they were much warmer. This would do just fine.

He let out a wide, squeaky yawn. Then he twisted around until he found a comfortable position. This was an even better place to sleep than his rock cave had been. Snuggling against the thick blankets was – almost – like being with his family again.

He yawned again and rested his head on his front paws. Then, almost before he had time to close his eyes, he was sound asleep.

It had been a very eventful day.

The blankets were so comfortable that he slept well into the morning. When he opened his eyes, he felt too lazy to get up. He stretched out all four paws and gave himself a little "good morning" woof.

Food would be nice. He crawled out from

underneath the heavy blankets. The sun was shining and the sky was bright and clear. The ocean was only a couple of blocks away, and he could smell the fresh, salty air. Oceanport was at its best on days like this.

Instead of jumping down, he kept sitting in the sleigh for a while. Being up so high was fun. He could see lots of cars driving by, and people walking around to do their errands. He kept his nose in the wind, smelling all sorts of intriguing smells.

A sanitation worker named Joseph Robinson, who was emptying the corner litter basket, was the first person to notice him.

"Hey, check it out!" he said to his colleague. "It's Santa Paws!"

His colleague, Maria, followed his gaze and laughed. "I wish I had a camera," she said.

The town postman, Rasheed, who was passing by on his morning delivery route, overheard them. "Santa Paws?" he repeated, not sure if he had heard right.

Joseph and Maria pointed at the dog sitting up in the sleigh.

Rasheed shook his head in amusement.

"That *is* pretty goofy." He shook his head again. "Santa Paws. I like that."

Then they all went back to work, still smiling.

Unaware of that whole conversation, the dog enjoyed his high perch for a while longer before jumping down. It was time to find something good to eat.

There was a doughnut shop at the corner of Tidewater Road and Main Street. The dog nosed through the rubbish bins in the back. Finally, he unearthed a box of biscuits that had been discarded because they were past the freshness deadline. To him, they tasted just fine. A little dry, maybe.

From there, he went to the ever-leaking drainpipe behind the pizza place and drank his fill. There was so much ice now that the flow was slowing down, but he was still able to satisfy his thirst. He cut his tongue slightly on the jagged edge of the pipe and had to whimper a few times. But then, he went straight back to drinking.

With breakfast out of the way, he decided to make the rounds. The middle school would be his last stop. He visited all of his usual places, neither seeing – nor smelling – anything terribly interesting. It was three days before Christmas, and everything in Oceanport seemed to be just fine.

He was ambling down Meadowlark Way when he noticed something unusual in the road. To be precise, there were cows *everywhere*. Lots and lots of *cows*.

He stopped, his ears moving straight up. He had seen cows before, but never up close. They were *big*. Their hooves looked sharp, too. Dangerous.

The cows belonged to the Jorgensens, who owned a small family farm. They sold milk, and eggs, and tomatoes, in season. The weight of all of the snow had been too much for one section of their fence, and the cows had wandered through the opening. Now they were all standing in the middle of the street, mooing pensively and looking rather lost.

The dog's first instinct was to bark, so he did. Most of the cows looked up, and then shuffled a few feet down the road. Then they all stood around some more.

OK. If he kept barking, they would probably

keep moving, but he wasn't sure if that's what he wanted them to do. Except they were in the middle of the road. They were *in his way*. And what if scary cars came? That would be bad.

He barked again, experimentally, and the cows clustered closer together. They looked at him; he looked at them.

Now what? The dog barked a very fierce bark and the cows started shuffling down the lane. The more he barked, the faster they went. In fact it was sort of fun.

The cows seemed to know where they were going, and the dog followed along behind. If they slowed down, he would bark. Once, they sped up too much, and he had to race up ahead. Then he skidded to a stop and barked loudly at them.

The cows stopped, and turned to go back the other way. That didn't seem right at all, so the dog ran back behind them. He barked a rough, tough bark, and even threw in a couple of growls for good measure.

With a certain amount of confusion, the cows faced forward again. Relieved, the dog barked more pleasantly, and they all resumed their journey down the road. He didn't know where they were going, but at least they were making progress.

When they came to a long driveway, the cows all turned into it. The dog was a little perplexed by this, but the cows seemed pretty sure of themselves. He barked until they got to the end of the driveway where there was a sprawling old farmhouse and a big wooden barn.

The cows all clustered up by the side of the barn, and mooed plaintively. The dog ran back and forth in a semicircle around them, trying to keep all of them in place. If he barked some more, who knew *where* they might go next.

A skinny woman wearing overalls and a hooded parka came out of the barn. She stared at the scene, and then leaned inside the barn. "Mortimer," she bellowed in a voice that sounded too big for someone so slim. "Come here! Something very strange has happened."

Her husband, who had a big blond beard, appeared in the doorway, holding a pitchfork.

"What is it, Yolanda?" he asked vaguely. "Did I leave the iron on again?"

"Look, Morty," she said, and pointed. "*The cows came home*."

He thought about that, and then frowned. "Weird," he said, and went back into the barn.

Yolanda rolled her eyes in annoyance. There was a fenced-in paddock outside the barn and she went over to unlatch the gate. "Come on, you silly cows," she said, swinging the gate open. "You've caused more than enough trouble for one day. Let's go."

The cows didn't budge.

"Great," she said. She turned and whistled in the direction of the barn.

After a minute, a very plump Border collie loped obediently outside.

"Good girl," Yolanda praised her. "Herd, girl!"

The Border collie snapped into action. She darted over to the cows, her body low to the ground. She barked sharply, and herded them into a compact group.

Wanting to help, the dog barked, too. The

Border collie didn't seem to want any inter-ference and even snapped at him once, but when she drove the cows towards the open gate, he ran along behind her. It was almost like being with his mother again. *She* liked him to stay out of the way when she was busy, too.

One cow veered away from the others, and the Border collie moved more swiftly than seemed to be physically possible for such a fat dog. She nipped lightly at the cow's hooves and nudged it back into the group.

Imitating her, the dog kept the cows on the other side in line. Whatever the Border collie did, he would promptly mimic. In no time, the cows were safely in the paddock.

"Good girl, Daffodil," Yolanda said, and handed the Border collie a biscuit from her coat pocket. "That's my little buttercup."

The Border collie wagged her tail and waddled off to eat her treat.

The biscuit smelled wonderful. The dog sat down and politely lifted his paw. Maybe he would get one, too.

"Yeah, I think you've earned one," Yolanda

said, and tossed him a Milk-Bone. "Whoever you are."

He had never had a Milk-Bone before, but he liked it a lot. Nice and crunchy. When he was finished, he barked.

"No, just one," Yolanda told him. "Run along now. I have work to do."

The dog barked, trotted partway down the driveway, and trotted back.

"Oh." Yolanda suddenly understood what he was trying to tell her. "The cows had to come from *somewhere*, didn't they? I bet there's a big hole in the fence." She turned towards the barn. "Mortimer! The fence is down again! We have to go and fix it!"

"OK. You do that, honey," he called back.

"It doesn't sound like he's going to *help* me, now does it," she said to the dog.

The dog cocked his head.

"*Men*," Yolanda pronounced with great disgust, and went to get her tools.

The dog led her down the road to the broken spot.

"Well, how about that," she said. She bent down and lifted the fallen fence post. Then she pounded it back in place. "I don't suppose you want to stay," she said conversationally. "Our Daffodil would probably like some help herding."

Stay. He had heard "Stay" before. It meant *something*, but he wasn't sure what. He rolled over a couple of times, to be cooperative, but she didn't even notice. So he just sat down to wait for her to finish. Maybe she would give him another one of those good biscuits.

Yolanda hefted the two wooden bars that had collapsed and slid them into place. "There we go!" she said, and brushed her hands off triumphantly. She reached into her pocket for another Milk-Bone and held it out. "Here's your reward."

The dog barked happily and took the biscuit. Then he headed down the road, carrying it in his mouth. He had places to go, things to do — and a school to visit!

"Well, wait a minute," Yolanda protested. "You don't have to go, you can —"

The dog had already disappeared around the curve and out of sight.

Chapter 10

It was fun to walk along carrying his biscuit, like he was a *real* dog, with a *real* owner, who loved him. But soon, he couldn't resist stopping and eating it.

When he got to the middle school, the building was deserted. No cars, no buses, no teachers, no students, no Mrs Gustave.

No Patricia, no Oscar, no *Gregory*.

Where was everyone? They should be here!

He slumped down right where he was and lay in a miserable heap. Maybe they had gone away for ever, the way his family had. Why did everyone keep leaving him?

He stayed there on the icy front walk until his body was stiff from the cold. Then he got up and slunk around to the back of the building. Maybe he would be able to find some rubbish to eat.

When he passed his little sleeping alcove by the playground, he caught a fresh scent. Gregory and Oscar had been here! Not too long ago! He ran into the alcove and found a big red dish full of some dark meaty food. What was it? There were lots of chunks and different flavours. It tasted soft and delicious, like a *special* food, made just for dogs. It was *great*.

Next to the red dish, there was a yellow dish full of water. The top had frozen, but he slapped his paw against it, and the ice shattered. He broke a hole big enough for his muzzle to fit through. Then he drank at least half of the water in the bowl in one fell swoop.

What a nice surprise! Food *and* water! They hadn't forgotten him, after all.

If he waited long enough, maybe they would come again. He lay down next to the dishes and watched the empty playground with his alert brown eyes.

Several hours passed, but no one came. He

still lay where he was, on full-alert, without moving. A couple of birds flew by. A squirrel climbed from one tree to another, and then disappeared inside a hole. A big chunk of ice fell off the school roof, landing nearby.

That was it.

Maybe they had just come back *once*, and never would again. Maybe he was doomed to be alone for ever.

Discouraged, the dog dragged himself to his feet. His back itched, but he was too sad to bother scratching. It would take too much energy.

He wandered off in a new direction, exploring a different part of town. Soon, he came upon the largest car park he had ever seen. There were only a few cars in it, but the smell of exhaust fumes was so strong that there must have been many other cars here, not too long ago. He marked several places, just to cover up the ugly stench of petrol and oil.

The car park went on and on and on. It seemed endless. In the middle, there were a lot of low buildings. They were different sizes, but they seemed to be attached.

He walked closer, sniffing the air curiously. *Many* people had been walking around here. Recently. There were food smells, too. His feet touched a rubber mat, and to his amazement, two glass doors swung open in front of him.

Alarmed, he backed away. Why did the doors open like that? For no good reason?

Gingerly, he stepped on the mat again – and the doors opened again! Since it seemed to be all right, he walked cautiously through the doors and inside.

It was a very strange place. There was a wide open space in the centre, with lots of benches scattered around. Water bubbled inside a big fountain, and the lights were very dim. He could smell the sharp odour of industrial cleaner, and hear people talking about a hundred feet away. A radio was playing somewhere, too.

He wasn't sure if he liked this place, but then he saw a sleigh. It was just like the one in the park! He wagged his tail, and happily leaped inside. Mounds of soft cloth were tucked around the cardboard presents in the back. He wiggled around until he had made enough room to sleep among the boxes. This was even *better* than the sleigh in the park!

He yawned and rolled on to his back. Sometimes he liked to sleep with his feet up in the air. It was restful.

Off to the side of the Santa Claus display, two cleaners walked by with mops and pails. Hearing them, the dog crouched down in the sleigh. This was *such* a nice place to sleep that he didn't want them to see him. In the dark, they probably wouldn't, but he wanted to be sure.

"You two about finished?" a woman called to the two men.

"Yeah!" one of the cleaners answered. "The food court was a real mess, though."

The woman, who was their supervisor, walked down the mall with a clipboard in her hand. "Well, let's lock up those last two electric doors, and get out of here. We open at nine tomorrow, and this place is going to be *packed* with all the last-minute shoppers."

The other cleaner groaned. "I'm glad Christmas only comes once a year."

"Wait until the after-Christmas sales," his partner said glumly. "That's even crazier."

Their supervisor shrugged, making ticking marks on her clipboard. "Hey, with this economy, we should just be *glad* to have the business." She tucked the clipboard under her arm. "Come on. We'll go and check in with the security people, and then you two can take off."

As they walked away, the dog relaxed. It looked like he was safe. He yawned again, shut his eyes, and went to sleep with no trouble whatsoever.

During the night, he would hear someone walk by every so often, along with the sound of keys clanking. But he just stayed low, and the guards would pass right by without noticing him. He got up a couple of times to lift his leg against a big, weird plant, but then went back to bed each time. It was morning now, but he was happy to sleep late.

Then, a lot of people came, and he could hear metal gates sliding up all over the place. Different kinds of food started cooking somewhere nearby, and Christmas music began to play loudly.

He started to venture out, but he was afraid. What would happen if the people saw him? Maybe he *shouldn't* have come in here, after all. It might have been bad.

Suddenly, the weight of the sleigh shifted as a hefty man sat down on the wide vinyl bench in the front. He was wearing a big red suit with a broad black belt, and he smelled strongly of coffee and bacon.

The dog scrunched further back into the presents. He wanted to panic and run away, but for now, he decided to stay hidden. There were just too many people around.

"Ready for another long day of dandling tots on your lap, Chet?" a man standing next to the sleigh said.

All decked out in his Santa Claus costume, Chet looked tired already. "Oh, yeah," he said. "I *love* being Santa."

"Rather you than me," the man said, and moved on to open up his sporting goods store.

Soon, there were people *everywhere*. So many people that the dog quivered with fear as he hid under the soft layers of red and green felt. All of the voices, and music, and twinkling lights were too much for him to take. Too many sounds. Too many *smells*. He closed his eyes, and tried to sleep some more. For once in his life, it was *difficult*.

Tiny children kept getting in and out of the sleigh. They would talk and talk, and Chet would bounce them on his big red knee. Sometimes, they cried, and every so often, a bright light would flash.

It was *horrible*. And – he had to go to the toilet again. Could he go on the presents, or would that be bad? He would try to wait.

Unknown to the dog, Gregory and Patricia Callahan had come to the mall with their mother. They still had some presents to buy, and the next day was Christmas Eve. Mrs Callahan had told them that they could each bring along a friend. So Gregory invited Oscar, and Patricia called up *her* best friend, Rachel. Mrs Callahan was going to buy all of them lunch and then, if they behaved, they would get to go to a movie later.

"I'm going to have a burrito," Gregory decided as they walked along.

His mother looked up from her lengthy

Christmas list. Mrs Callahan taught physics at the high school, so she had had to do most of her shopping on the weekends. She had been doing her best, but she was still very far behind. She was a woman of *science*, but not necessarily one of precision.

"We've just had breakfast, Greg," she said. "Besides, I thought you wanted sweet and sour chicken."

"Dad said we could order in Chinese tonight," Gregory reminded her. "So he could finish his chapter, instead of cooking."

"Pizza," Patricia said flatly. "Pizza's *much* better."

Hearing that, their mother stopped walking. "If you two start fighting…"

They gave her angelic smiles.

"Never, *ever*, Mummy," Gregory promised, trying to sound sweet.

"We *love* each other," Patricia agreed.

Then, when their mother turned her back, Gregory gave his sister a shove. Patricia retaliated with a quick kick to his right shin. Gregory bit back a groan, and hopped for a few feet until it stopped hurting.

"Do you think the dog ever came back?" Oscar asked him, as they paused to admire the window of the computer shop.

Gregory shrugged. "I hope so. If we keep leaving food, he'll know he can trust us. Then we'll be able to catch him."

"What did your parents say?" Rachel asked, tapping the floor just ahead of her with her cane. She had been blind since she was four, but she got around so well that they all usually forgot about it. Her eyes hadn't been physically scarred, but she still *always* wore sunglasses. If people asked, she would explain that it was "a coolness thing". No one who knew the two of them was surprised that she and Patricia had been best friends since kindergarten. "Do you think they'll let you bring him home?" she asked.

"Well – we're working on them," Patricia assured her. "They still really miss Marty, so I think they want to wait a while before we get another dog." Then she touched her friend's arm lightly. "Rubbish bin, at nine o'clock."

Rachel nodded and moved to avoid the obstacle.

"Next year, you're old enough to get a dog, right?" Gregory said, meaning a guide dog.

Rachel nodded. "I can't wait. Except I have to *stay* at that school for a while, to learn how. Live away from home."

Patricia shrugged. "It's not so far. We can come and visit you."

Rachel pretended to be disgusted by that idea. "And that would be a *good* thing?"

"For *you*," Patricia said, and they both laughed.

"Those guide dogs are really smart," Gregory said, and paused. "Although not as smart as *my* new dog is going to be. He's the best dog *ever*."

Oscar snorted. "Oh, yeah. He's a whiz, all right." He turned towards Patricia and Rachel. "Fetches *snowballs*, that dog."

The girls laughed again.

"Well, that makes him about Gregory's speed," Rachel said.

"Absolutely," Patricia agreed. "He doesn't even know how to *sit* right." She glanced a few feet ahead. "Baby carriage, two o'clock," she said, and then went on without pausing.

"Rachel, you're going to have to help me train him, so he won't *embarrass* us."

Rachel grinned, tapping her cane and deftly avoiding the baby carriage. "You mean, Gregory, or the dog?"

"*Gregory*, of course," Patricia said.

"What if he never comes back?" Oscar said. "I mean, he might belong to someone, or – I don't know. He could be really far away by now."

Gregory looked worried. He was so excited about the dog that he had forgotten that he might not even see him again. Someone else might find him, or he might get hurt, or – all sorts of terrible things could happen! The worst part would be that he would never even *know* why the dog hadn't come back. He would just be – gone.

"Cheer up, Greg," Patricia said. "He's probably still hanging around the school. I mean, he didn't exactly seem like, you know, a dog with a lot of *resources*."

Gregory just looked worried.

"Are you kids coming or not?" Mrs Callahan asked, about ten feet ahead of them.

"We have a lot of stops to make."

They all nodded, and hurried to catch up.

Down in front of the Thom McAn shoe shop, a young father was trying to balance a bunch of bulging shopping bags and a push-chair, which held his two-year-old son, Kyle. At the same time, he was trying to keep track of his other three children, who were four, six and seven. His wife was down in the Walden book shop, and they were all supposed to meet in the food court in half an hour.

"Lucy, watch it," he said to his six-year-old as she bounced up and down in place, croaking. She was pretending to be a frog. His four-year-old, Marc, was singing to himself, while the seven-year-old, Wanda, was trying to peek inside the Toys R Us bags. "Wanda, put that down! Marc, will you –" He stopped, realizing that the push-chair was empty. "Kyle? Where's Kyle?"

The other three children stopped what they were doing.

"I haven't seen him, Daddy," Wanda said. "Honest."

The other two just looked scared.

Their father spun around, searching the crowd frantically. "Kyle?" he shouted. "Where are you? Kyle, come back here!"

His two-year-old was missing!

Chapter 11

Immediately, a crowd gathered around the family. Everyone was very concerned, and spread out to look for the lost little boy. The mall security guards showed up, and quickly ran to block of all of the exits. Children got lost at the mall all the time, and the guards just wanted to make sure that when it happened, they didn't *leave* the mall.

"What's going on?" Mrs Callahan asked, as they came out of the Sharper Image shop. One of her contact lenses had fogged up a little, and she blinked to clear it.

"Oh, no!" Patricia said, with great drama. "Maybe it's a run on the bank!"

"You mean, a run on the cash machines," Rachel corrected her.

"Maybe there's a movie star here or something," Oscar guessed. "Someone *famous*."

That idea appealed to Gregory, and he looked around in every direction. "What if it was someone like Michael Jordan," he said. "That'd be great!"

"*Shaquille*," Oscar said, and they bumped chests in the same dumb-jock way basketball players did.

Mrs Callahan reached out to stop a woman in a pink hat who was rushing by. "Excuse me," she said. "What's going on?"

"A little boy is lost," the woman told her. "Curly hair, two years old, wearing a Red Sox jacket. They can't find him anywhere!"

"Can we look, Mum?" Gregory asked.

"We'll look *together*," Mrs Callahan said firmly. "I don't want us to get separated in this crowd."

Up in the sleigh, the dog had heard all of the sudden chaos, too. The noise had woken him up. What was going on? Why was everyone so upset? He couldn't resist poking his head up and looking around. People were running around all over the place, and shouting, "Kyle! Kyle! Where are you, Kyle?"

The dog didn't know what to think. But, once again, he was sure that something was very wrong. Then, amidst all of the uproar, he heard a distinct little sound. A strange sound. He stood up in the sleigh and pricked his ears forward, listening intently.

It had been a *splash*. Now, he could hear a tiny *gurgle*. Where was it coming from? The fountain. Something – some*one*? – must have fallen into the huge, bubbling fountain in the middle of the mall. The dog stood there indecisively. What should he do? Run away? Run to the *fountain*? Stay here?

A man searching for Kyle right near the sleigh stared at him. It was Rasheed, the postman, who had seen the dog in the park the day before – sitting up in Santa's sleigh. The dog that Joseph, the sanitation worker, had called Santa Paws.

Rasheed had come to the mall on his day off to buy some presents for his colleagues. This was certainly the *last* place he would have expected to see that dog.

"Look at that!" he gasped to his wife, who

was standing next to him. "It's Santa Paws!"

She looked confused. "What?"

"Santa Paws!" he said, pointing up at the sleigh.

The dog had his full concentration on the distant fountain. There was something *in* there. Under the water. Movement. It was – a child! A drowning child!

He sailed off the sleigh in one great leap. Then he galloped through the crowded mall as fast as he could. The top of the fountain was very high, but he gathered his legs beneath him and sprang off the ground.

He landed in the fountain with a huge splash and water splattered everywhere. He dug frantically through the water with his paws, searching for the child.

By now, Kyle had sunk lifelessly to the bottom of the fountain. The dog dived underneath the churning water and grabbed the boy's jacket between his teeth. Then he swam furiously to the surface, using all of his strength to pull the boy along behind him.

All at once, both of their heads popped up. Kyle started choking weakly, and the dog dragged him to the edge of the fountain. He tried to pull him over the side, but the little boy was too heavy, and the dog was too small. He tightened his jaws on the boy's jacket, and tried again. But it was no use. The edge of the fountain was just too high.

The dog used his body to keep the little boy pressed safely against the side of the fountain. Then he started barking, as he dog-paddled to try and keep them both afloat.

"I hear a dog barking," one of the security guards yelled. "Where's it coming from? Someone find that dog!"

In the meantime, Rasheed was running down the mall towards the fountain.

"In there!" he panted, gesturing towards the fountain. "The little boy's in there! Don't worry, Santa Paws has him!"

Even in the midst of all the excitement, people stared at him when they heard the name, "Santa Paws".

"Santa *Paws*?" the security guard repeated. "Well. Hmmm. I think you mean –"

Rasheed ignored him, climbing over the side of the fountain. He plucked Kyle out of the water and lifted him to safety. Everyone nearby began to clap.

"Is he all right?" Kyle's father asked, frantic with worry. "Oh, please, tell me he's all right?"

Kyle was coughing and choking, but fully conscious. He would be just fine. Very carefully, Rasheed climbed back over the side of the fountain, holding the little boy in his arms.

Kyle's sisters and brother promptly burst into tears.

"Oh, *thank you*, sir," Kyle's father said, picking up his wet son in a big hug. Kyle started crying, too, and hung on to him tightly. "I don't know how I can ever thank you," his father went on.

"It wasn't me," Rasheed said. "It was Santa Paws."

All of the people who had gathered by the fountain to watch stared at him.

"Are you new to this country?" one of them asked tentatively. "Here, in America, we call him Santa *Claus*."

Rasheed looked irritated. "Oh, give me a break," he said, sounding impatient. "I'm *third-generation.*"

Now, the dog struggled over the edge of the fountain. He jumped down to the wet pavement and shook thoroughly. Water sprayed all over the place.

"*There's* your hero," Rasheed proclaimed proudly. "It's Santa Paws!"

Everyone clapped again.

Several stores away, still trying to get through the crowd, Gregory saw the dog. Instantly, he grabbed his mother's arm.

"Mum, that's him!" he said eagerly. "My dog! Isn't he great? Can we keep him? Please?"

His mother shook her head, not sure if she could believe the coincidence. "What? Are you sure?" she asked. "Here, in the *mall?*"

"That's the dog!" Gregory insisted. "The one we want to come and live with us!"

"That's no dog," a woman next to them said solemnly. "That's *Santa Paws!*"

"He just saved that little boy," one of the workers from the taco stand agreed. "He's a hero!"

Patricia looked disgusted. "*Santa Paws?*" she said. "What a *completely* dumb name."

Rachel nodded. "It's embarrassing. It's…" – she paused for effect – "not cool."

Patricia nodded, too. It wasn't cool *at all*.

"I have to get him!" Gregory said, and started trying to push his way through the crowd.

Down by the fountain, the dog was shrinking away from all of the people and attention. Everyone was trying to touch him and pat him at once. There were too many people. Too much noise. Too much *everything*.

So unexpectedly that everyone was startled, the dog raced away from them.

"Someone catch him!" Kyle's father shouted. "He saved my little boy!"

People started chasing the dog, but he was much too fast. He ran until he found one of the rubber mats and then jumped on it. The doors opened and he tore out of the mall. He raced through the car park, dodging cars and customers.

It was a scary place, and he was never going back!

Inside the mall, Gregory got to the fountain only seconds after the dog had left.

"Where's my dog?" he asked urgently. "I mean – where's Santa Paws!"

Everyone turned and pointed to the exit.

"Thanks!" Gregory said, and ran in that direction. But when he got outside, the dog was already long gone.

Disappointed, he walked slowly back inside. He had *almost* got him, this time. What if he never got another chance?

Oscar caught up with him. "Where'd he go? Is he still here?"

Gregory shook his head unhappily. "Lost him again. What if he disappears for good, this time?"

"I'm sorry," Oscar said. Then he threw a comforting arm around his friend's shoulders. "Don't worry. We'll find him again. Count on it."

"I sure *hope* so," Gregory said glumly.

Just then, Kyle's mother came walking up to the fountain. She was carrying lots of bags and whistling a little. She gave her husband and children a big smile.

"Well, *there* you are," she said. "I've been waiting in the food court *for ever* – I was starting to worry."

Then, seeing the large crowd around her family, she frowned.

"Did I miss something?" she asked.

Everyone just groaned.

Chapter 12

The name "Santa Paws" caught on, and news of the hero dog spread quickly all over Oceanport. People began coming forward with tales about *their* experiences with Santa Paws. Some of these stories were more plausible than others. There were people who thought that a stray dog on his own might be wild – and possibly dangerous. They thought that he should be caught, and taken to the pound as soon as possible. One man even claimed that Santa Paws had growled viciously at him on Hawthorne Street, but since he was a Yankees fan living in the middle of New England, nobody took him very seriously.

Most of the town was behind Santa Paws

one hundred per cent. Officers Bronkowski and Lee told how the dog had scared the vandals away from the Nativity scene. Mrs Amory spoke from her hospital bed about how he had saved her life when she fell on the ice and broke her hip. Yolanda's husband Mortimer said, vaguely, "Oh, yeah, that was the weird dog who brought the cows home." One woman said that Santa Paws had magically cleared the snow from her front walk and driveway earlier that week. Another family claimed that he had been up on the roof and suddenly their television reception was much better. A little girl in the first grade was *sure* that he had come into her room while she was asleep and chased the monsters from her closet.

By now, the dog's brother and sisters and mother had all been adopted. Seeing the strong resemblance, their new owners were boasting that they owned dogs who might be *related* to the great Santa Paws. Although they had originally just gone to the pound to adopt nice stray dogs, these owners now felt very lucky, indeed.

In short, Santa Paws was the talk of the town. There was even a group who hung out at Sally's Diner & Sundries Shop taking bets on when, and where, Santa Paws might show up next. What heroic acts he would perform. Everyone who came into the diner had an enthusiastic prediction.

The newscasters on television had set up a Santa Paws hotline so people could phone in sightings. He was described as being small, and brown, and very, very wise.

In the meantime, the poor dog had barely stopped running since he had left the mall. He ran and ran and ran. He had got so wet from diving into the fountain that his fur froze. No matter what he did, he couldn't get warm. He ended up huddling against a tree in some waste ground as his body shook uncontrollably from the cold. He was glad that the little boy hadn't drowned, but it had still been a bad, scary day.

He was so tired and cold that he felt like giving up. He didn't *like* being on his own. It was too hard. He wanted a home. He wanted a family. He wanted to feel *safe*.

Instead, he sat in the waste ground all by himself and shivered. Every few minutes, he whimpered a little, too.

He was just plain *miserable*.

The same afternoon, Mrs Callahan let Gregory and Oscar skip going to the movies and leave the mall early. As long as they got home before dark, they had permission to go over to the school and leave some more food and water for the dog. If they could catch him, she said, Gregory could bring him home.

Gregory was overjoyed. Getting to keep the dog would be the best Christmas present he ever had! He just prayed that the dog would be there waiting for him. If not – well, he didn't want to think about the possibility of never finding him again. His parents would probably take him to the pound in a couple of weeks to get a different dog – but the *only* dog he wanted was Santa Paws. He had to be over at the school, he *just* had to be.

So, he and Oscar gathered up some supplies. Then Gregory's father left his word processor long enough to drive them over to the school. Gregory and Oscar were in such good moods that they didn't even complain when Mr Callahan made them listen to Frank Sinatra on the radio. They also didn't laugh when Mr Callahan sang along. Much.

Just as the chorus from "New York, New York" was over, Mr Callahan pulled up in front of the school. When he is in the middle of a new book, he was sometimes very absentminded. Today, he still had on his bunny slippers. Gregory and Oscar were afraid that they would laugh more, so they pretended not to notice.

"OK, guys," Mr Callahan said, as he parked the car. "You want me to wait, or would you rather walk home?"

Gregory and Oscar looked at each other.

"Would we have to listen to more Sinatra, Mr Callahan?" Oscar asked politely.

Gregory's father nodded. He was tall and a little bit pudgy, with greying hair and thick horn-rimmed glasses. "I'm afraid so," he said.

"Well, then," Oscar answered, very politely, "maybe it would be very good exercise for us to walk."

"Thanks for driving us, though," Gregory added.

Mr Callahan grinned, raised the volume on the radio, and drove away. He beeped the horn twice, waved, and then turned on to the main road to head home.

"For Christmas, you should give him a CD of *good* music," Oscar said. "So he'll know what it sounds like."

Gregory laughed. His father's idea of modern music was the Eagles. Mr Callahan liked the Doobie Brothers, too.

He and Oscar had brought more dog food, some biscuits, a couple of thick beach towels, and a new collar and leash. Gregory was also carrying a big cardboard box the dog could use for shelter, in case they missed him again. He hoped that as long as they kept leaving things, the dog would keep coming back.

When they got to the little alcove, they saw that all of the food was gone. Most of the water was, too.

"Good!" Gregory said happily. "He found it!" He would have been very sad if the bowls hadn't been touched.

Oscar nodded, bending down to refill the water dish. "I hope so. I mean, I wouldn't want *other* dogs to be eating his food."

Now, Gregory frowned. "Whoa. I didn't even think of that."

Oscar shrugged. "Don't worry. It was probably him, anyway." Then he took out a big can of dog food. To open it, he used a special little can opener his father had had in Vietnam. Oscar was very proud that his father had given it to him, and he always carried it on his key chain.

Gregory set up the cardboard box in the most protected corner. It had come from some catalogue when his mother ordered new duvets, so it was pretty big. Then he packed some snow against the side, so it wouldn't blow away. Right now, the wind wasn't blowing very hard, but it might pick up later.

"On the top, too," Oscar advised. "Just in case."

Gregory considered that, and then frowned. The box was *only* made of cardboard. "Maybe a little. I don't want it to collapse."

"It might be good insulation, though,"

Oscar said.

That made sense, so Gregory did it. Then he folded the beach towels and put them neatly inside. One was yellow, and the other had a faded Bugs Bunny on it. He arranged them until they formed a nice, warm bed. He had also brought three dog biscuits, and he laid them out in a row on the top towel. That way, the dog could have a bedtime snack.

"Think he'll like this?" he asked.

Oscar nodded. "Totally." He put his key chain back in his pocket and dumped the dog food into the big red dish. "I think he'll be really happy."

"Me, too," Gregory agreed. What he wanted more than anything was for the dog to feel *special*. Loved.

Once they had set everything up, they sat down in the snow to wait for a while. If they were lucky, maybe the dog would show up. If not, tomorrow was Christmas Eve, and they had a whole week of holiday vacation ahead. They could come here and wait around all day, every day, if they wanted. He would have to come back at some point – wouldn't he?

It was pretty cold, sitting there in the snow, but they stayed for over an hour. The dog was probably busy saving people somewhere. Oscar searched his jacket pockets and found a deck of cards. To pass the time, they played Hearts, and Go Fish, and Old Maid.

The sun was starting to go down, and shadows were creeping across the playground.

Gregory sighed. "We'd better go. We promised we'd get home before dark."

Oscar nodded and stood up. He put his cards in the pocket of his Bruins jacket, and brushed the snow off his jeans. "Don't worry, Greg. We'll just keep coming back until we find him."

"What if someone *else* finds him?" Gregory asked. Now that Santa Paws was famous, *everyone* was going to want him.

"*Nobody* is going to think to look here," Oscar pointed out. "Nobody."

Gregory sure hoped not.

The dog quivered against the tree in the waste ground for a long time. The ice particles in his fur felt sharp. He couldn't remember ever feeling so uncomfortable. He was very hungry, too. He was *always* hungry.

He was also still scared from having been in the big place with all those people. He didn't like the noise, or all the unfamiliar faces staring at him. He *never* wanted to go to a place like that again.

He was very hungry. If he started walking around again, he might find some more food. Maybe it would also seem warmer if he kept moving.

He was afraid of running into strangers, so he waited until it was dark. Then he waited until he didn't hear any cars going by. Finally, he got up enough nerve to leave the waste ground.

He decided to travel along side roads and back alleys. It might be safer. He took a route that went along the ocean, so that he could avoid the centre of town.

The dog walked very slowly along Overlook Drive. His paws hurt. He was hungry and thirsty. There was still lots of ice on his coat. Instead of carrying his tail up jauntily, the way he usually did, he let it drag behind him.

He just wasn't feeling very happy right now.

He wandered unhappily off the road and down to the beach in the dark. The cold sand felt strange under his paws, but he kind of liked it. He kept slipping and sliding.

The water was very noisy. It was almost high tide, and big waves were rolling in and out. The dog trotted down to the edge of the water to drink some.

Just as he put his head down, foamy water came rushing towards him. He yelped in surprise and jumped out of the way. Why did the water *move* like that?

He waited for a minute, and then tried again. The water rushed in his direction, almost knocking him off his feet. And it was cold!

He ran back on to the dry sand and shook himself vigorously. It was like the water was *playing* with him. He decided that it would be fun to join the game. A lot more fun than feeling sad. So he chased the waves back and forth until he got tired.

A flock of seagulls flew past him in the night sky and he barked happily at them.

This was a nice place, even though the water smelled sort of funny. He tasted some and then made gagging noises. It was awful!

The taste in his mouth was so sour and salty that he lost interest in chasing the waves. It was too cold, anyway.

He trotted along the sand until he came to a big stone seawall. It took him three tries, but he finally managed to scramble over it. He landed hard on the icy pavement on the other side with his legs all splayed out. It hurt. But he picked himself up and only limped for about three metres. Then he forgot that he had hurt himself at all, and went back to trotting.

Fifteen minutes later, the dog found himself at the middle school. He paused at the rubbish bins and lifted his nose in the air for a hopeful sniff. Even if he could have reached the rubbish, what little there was smelled rotten.

Even so, his stomach churned with hunger. When had he eaten last? That nice meaty food yesterday? It had been so good that he could *still* almost taste it.

He ran behind the school to the play-ground. He stopped before he got to the alcove, and whined a little. If there wasn't any food there, he was going to be very disappointed. What if they had forgotten him?

He took his time walking over, pausing every few steps and whining softly. Then he caught a little whiff of that special meaty smell. There *was* food waiting for him!

He raced into the alcove so swiftly that he almost knocked the dishes over. Food and water! All for him! He *loved* Gregory and Oscar. There was another familiar smell, too. He sniffed a few more times and then barked with delight.

Milk-Bones!

The dog was very happy when he went to sleep that night.

Chapter 13

The next day was Christmas Eve. The sky was overcast and the temperature was just above freezing. But the dog had been warm and comfortable inside his cardboard box. The thick towels felt very soft and clean next to his body.

He had eaten one of the biscuits right before he went to sleep. His plan was to save the other two for the morning. But they smelled so good that he woke up in the middle of the night and crunched down one more.

When he woke up just before dawn, he yawned and stretched out all four paws. He liked his box-home a whole lot! There was still one biscuit left and he held it between his front paws. It was so nice to have his own bone that he just looked at it, wagging his tail.

Then he couldn't stand it any more, and he started crunching. It tasted just as good as the other two! He was so happy!

It was time to go outside. Feeling full of energy, he rolled to his feet. He hit his head against the top of the box, but that was OK. He *liked* that it was cosy. He yawned again and ambled outside.

His water bowl had frozen again. He jumped on the ice with his front paws, and it broke easily. He lapped up a few mouthfuls and then licked his chops. He could still taste the Milk-Bone, a little. It still tasted delicious!

He galloped around the playground twice to stretch his legs. Because he was happy, he barked a lot, too.

Would his friends come back soon? He sat down to wait. Then he got bored. So he rolled on his back for a while. But that got boring, too.

Next, he took a little nap until the sun rose. When he woke up, Gregory and Oscar still hadn't come. He was very restless, so he decided to go for a walk. Maybe he would go back to the beach and play with the moving water some more.

After about an hour of wandering, he walked up Prospect Street, near a little parade of shops. A girl was standing on the pavement without moving. She was holding a funny-looking stick, and she seemed worried.

It was Patricia's best friend Rachel. She was on her way to the 7-Eleven to pick up some milk and rye bread for her mother. Unfortunately, her wallet had fallen out of her pocket on the way, and now she couldn't find it.

She hated to ask people for help. So she was retracing her steps and using her red and white cane to feel for the missing object. She could go home and tell her mother what happened, but she would rather not. It wasn't that she was afraid someone would *steal* the wallet if she left. She just liked to do things by herself.

The dog cocked his head. Why was she moving *so slowly*? Why was she swinging the little stick around? He didn't want the stick to hit him, so he kept his distance.

"Now, where is it?" Rachel muttered. She bent down and felt the snow with her gloved hands. This was so frustrating! "Why can't I find the stupid thing?" she asked aloud.

The dog woofed softly.

Rachel stiffened. "Who's there?" she said, and got ready to use her cane as a weapon. She knew that it was a dog, but how could she be sure that it was friendly? Sometimes, dogs weren't.

The dog walked closer, wagging his tail.

Rachel felt something brush against her arm. The dog? She reached out and felt a wagging tail, and then a furry back.

"Are you a dog I know?" she asked.

Naturally, the dog didn't answer.

She took off her left glove and felt for the dog's collar. Her fingertips were so sensitive from reading Braille that she could usually read the inscriptions on licence tags. But this dog wasn't wearing a collar at all.

Could he be – Santa Paws? She ran her hand along his side and felt sharp ribs. He was *very* skinny. His fur felt rough and unbrushed, too. This dog had been outside for a very long time.

The dog liked the way she was patting him, so he licked her face.

"You're that dog Gregory's trying to catch, aren't you," Rachel said. "You must be."

The dog licked her face again.

It felt pretty slobbery, but Rachel didn't really mind. "Can you fetch?" she asked. "Or find? Do you know 'find'?"

The dog lifted his paw.

"I lost my wallet," she said. "I have to find it."

The dog barked and pawed at her arm.

"OK, OK." Rachel shook her head. Patricia was right – this dog needed some *serious* training. "Stay. I have to keep looking for it."

Stay. "Stay" meant something, but right now, the dog couldn't remember what. He barked uncertainly.

"*Stay*," she said over her shoulder.

He followed her as she kept retracing her steps. She would take a step, bend down and feel the snow and then take another step.

Was she looking for something? The dog sniffed around. The girl was walking so slowly that he leaped over a big drift to pass her. He could cover more ground that way.

He could smell that she had already walked on this part of the pavement. There were little bootsteps in the snow. He followed them until he smelled something else. He wasn't sure what it was, but the object had her scent on it. It was square and made of some kind of sturdy material.

So he picked the object up in his mouth and romped back up the street to where she was.

"I really can't play with you now," Rachel said, pushing him away. "I have to keep searching."

He pressed his muzzle against her arm, and then dropped the object in front of her.

Rachel heard it hit the ground and reached out to feel – her wallet!

"Good dog!" she said, and picked it up. "No wonder they call you Santa Paws. Good boy!"

The dog wagged his tail and woofed again. Rachel couldn't help wondering what he looked like. She had vague memories of things like colours and shapes. Mostly, though, she had to use her hands to picture things.

"Is it OK if I see what you look like?" she asked, surprised to find herself feeling shy. He was only a *dog*, even if he was a particularly good one.

The dog wagged his tail.

She put her hand out and felt the sharp ribs again. His fur was short and fairly dense. His winter undercoat, probably. The fur wasn't silky at all. Her family had a cocker spaniel named Trudy and she was very silky. This dog's fur was much more coarse.

The dog's hips were narrow, but his chest was pretty broad. Gregory had said that he wasn't full grown yet, but he was already at least forty or fifty pounds. He felt bony and athletic, not solid and stocky. That was the way her friend Gary's Labrador retriever felt. This dog was built differently.

She ran her hand down the dog's legs. They were very thin. His paws were surprisingly *big*. That meant Gregory was right, and the dog was going to grow a lot more.

She left his head for last. His ears seemed to be pointy, although they were a little crooked right at the very tip. His head and muzzle were long and slim. His mouth was open, but he was so gentle that she knew he wouldn't bite her.

"Thank you," she said, and removed her hands. She always felt better when she could *picture* something in her mind. She had a very clear picture, now, of this dog. A nice picture.

She was almost sure that the 7-Eleven was only about half a block away. There was a pay phone there. She should call Patricia's house right away and tell them to come and pick up the dog.

"Come here, Santa Paws," she said. "Just follow me down to this telephone, OK?"

There was no answering bark.

"Santa Paws?" she called. "Are you still here?"

She listened carefully, trying to hear him panting or the sound of his tail beating against the air. She could almost always sense it when any living being was near her.

The only thing she could sense right now was that the dog had gone away.

Rachel sighed. Oh, well. She could still call Patricia and tell her that the dog *had* been here. Briefly.

She wasn't sure if that would make Gregory feel better – or worse.

The dog's next stop was behind the doughnut shop. He checked the rubbish bins, but all he found were coffee grindings and crumpled napkins. He was more lucky at the pizza place, because he found a box full of discarded crusts. They were a little hard, but they tasted fine.

Now it was time to go to the beach. A couple of people shouted and pointed when they saw him, but he just picked up his pace. They sounded very excited to see him, but he had no idea why. So he kept running along until he outdistanced them.

Trotting down Harbour Cove Road, he heard several dogs barking and growling. They sounded like they were just around the next corner. He could also hear an elderly man shouting, "No, no! Bad dogs!" There was definitely trouble up ahead!

More alarmed than curious, he broke into a full run. He stretched his legs out as far as they would go, feeling the wind blow his ears back.

Just up ahead, at the base of an old oak tree, a big Irish setter, a Dalmatian and a husky-mix were all barking viciously. They had chased a kitten up the tree and were still yapping wildly at her from the bottom.

The elderly man, Mr Corcoran, was brandishing a stick and trying to make the dogs run away. The kitten belonged to him, and he loved her very much.

"Bad dogs!" he shouted. "Go home!"

The little kitten trembled up on the icy tree branch. Even though she was tiny, the branch was swaying under her weight and might break at any second.

The dog growled a warning, and then ran straight into the fray. He butted the Dalmatian in the side, and then shoved past the husky-mix, still growling.

At first, since he was obviously a puppy, the other dogs ignored him. They were having too much fun tormenting the kitten. The

Irish setter seemed to be the leader of the pack, so the puppy confronted him with a fierce bark.

This got the Irish setter's attention, but the puppy refused to back down. He showed his teeth and the Irish setter returned the favour. The Dalmatian and the husky-mix decided to join in, and the odds were three against one.

The dog was ready to fight *all* of them! He would probably lose, but he wasn't afraid. He stood his ground, trying to keep all three dogs in sight at once and not let any of them sneak up on him from behind. It was much harder than herding cows! And this time, Daffodil wasn't here to help him!

"Bad dogs!" Mr Corcoran yelled. "Leave him alone!"

Just as the husky-mix lunged towards the puppy, with her teeth bared, the kitten fell out of the tree with a shrieking meow. She landed in a clumsy heap in the snow, mewing pitifully.

Before the other dogs could hurt her, the puppy jumped past them, ready to protect her with his body. The other three dogs circled him slowly, planning their next moves. The puppy kept his teeth bared and growled steadily.

Swiftly and silently, the husky-mix leaped forward and bit his shoulder. The puppy yelped in pain, but snapped at one of the husky's back legs and heard the husky yelp, too.

Now the Irish setter moved in. At the last second, the puppy ducked and the setter sailed right over him. While the setter was trying to recover his balance, the puppy whirled around to face the Dalmatian.

The Dalmatian didn't like to fight, and he took one nervous step forward. Then he backed up, whining uneasily. The puppy made a short, fierce move towards him and the Dalmatian hesitated for a second. Then he tucked his tail between his legs and started running home.

Before the puppy had time to enjoy that victory, the Irish setter and the husky had already jumped on him. The puppy fought back, trying not to let them get between him and the mewing kitten.

He was ready to fight for his life — and the kitten's life!

Chapter 14

The fight was fast, confusing and brutal. "Stop it!" Mr Corcoran kept yelling helplessly. "Stop it right now!" He tried to break the fight up, using a stick he had found on the ground. It took a while, but he finally managed to knock the snarling husky away.

The husky growled at him, but then just limped off towards his owner's house. He had had enough fighting for one day.

Mrs Quigley, who lived across the street, came tearing outside in her bathrobe. "Pumpkin!" she shouted. "Bad dog, Pumpkin! You come here *right now*!"

Hearing the voice of authority, the Irish setter instantly cringed. Mrs Quigley grabbed him by the collar and hauled him away a few feet. "Bad, bad dog! You, *sit*!"

The Irish setter sat down, looking guilty.

"I'm so sorry, Carl," she said to Mr Corcoran, out of breath. "I don't know what could have got into him."

"*Eggnog*, probably," Mr Corcoran grumbled.

Mrs Quigley sniffed her dog's breath and then glared down at him. "Pumpkin! How could you? You bad, bad dog!" She looked up at Mr Corcoran. "I am so sorry. Are Matilda and your puppy all right?"

Mr Corcoran reached down and gently lifted his terrified kitten out of the snow. She was a calico cat, and her name was Matilda. He checked her all over, but except for being very frightened, she wasn't hurt.

"Oh, thank God," he said gratefully. "She's OK. I don't know what I would have done if they'd hurt her."

"I'm sorry," Mrs Quigley said, wringing her hands. "I promise I won't let Pumpkin get out like that again."

Hearing his name – and his owner's

disappointment – the Irish setter cringed lower. He was very ashamed.

In the meantime, feeling dazed, the puppy dragged himself to his feet. He hurt in a lot of places. He could feel blood on his left shoulder and his right ear was dripping blood, too. He had lots of other small cuts and slashes, but his ear and shoulder hurt the most. He shook his head from side to side, trying to clear away the dizziness.

Suddenly, Mrs Quigley looked horrified. "That isn't Santa Paws, is it?" she asked.

Mr Corcoran's eyes widened. "I don't know. I guess it could be. Who else would come to save Matilda?" He studied the dog more carefully. "The TV *did* say that he was small, and brown, and wise."

At that moment, the dog mainly looked *small*.

"Well, we're going to have to take him straight to the vet," Mrs Quigley said decisively. She aimed a stern finger at her Irish setter. "You are *very bad*, Pumpkin! You're going to have to go back to obedience school!"

The Irish setter wagged his tail tentatively

at the puppy. Now that the heat of the battle was over, he couldn't remember how, or why, the fight had started.

The puppy ignored him and tried to put weight on his injured shoulder. It hurt so much that he whimpered.

"Oh, you poor thing," Mrs Quigley cooed. "You just come here, snook'ums, and I'll take you to the vet."

The puppy veered away from her. He was in so much pain that he just wanted to be alone. Mrs Quigley and Mr Corcoran both tried to stop him, but he staggered off down the street. Then he forced himself into a limping run.

He wanted to get as far away from Harbour Cove Road as possible!

The dog only managed to run a couple of blocks before he had to stop. He lurched over to the side of the road and into the woods. His injured leg didn't want to work at all.

He collapsed next to an old tree stump. He rested on his bad side, and the snow numbed the pain a little. But it still hurt. A lot.

The dog whimpered and tried to lick the blood away from his wounds. He had never been in a fight with other dogs before. Dog fights were terrible! Especially when it was three against one!

His ear was stinging badly. He rubbed it against the snow to try and get rid of the pain. Instead, it started bleeding even more.

The dog whimpered pitifully and then closed his eyes. Right now, he was too weak to do anything else. Then, before he had a chance to fall asleep, he passed out.

It would be a long time before he woke up again.

Gregory and Oscar met on the school playground at ten-thirty. Patricia had insisted on coming along, too. Since the food was gone and the towels in the cardboard box were rumpled, they knew that the dog had been there. But he was gone now – and they had no way of knowing if he would ever come back.

"Where does he *go* every day?" Gregory asked, frustrated. "Doesn't he want us to find him?"

Oscar shrugged as he opened a brand-new can of dog food. "He's off doing hero stuff, probably."

Patricia didn't like to see the towels looking so messy. She bent down to refold them. "You know, that was really something at the mall," she remarked. "I've never seen a dog do anything like that before."

"He's not just any dog," Gregory said proudly.

Patricia nodded. For once, her brother was right. "I have to say, it was pretty cool." She reached into the open Milk-Bone box. "How many should I leave him?"

"Three," Gregory told her. "In a nice, neat row."

"Since it's Christmas Eve, let's give him four," Oscar suggested.

"Sounds good," Patricia said, and took out four biscuits.

When they were done, they sat down on a woollen blanket Oscar had brought. It was much more pleasant than sitting in the cold snow. Mrs Callahan had packed them a picnic lunch, too.

So they spent the next couple of hours eating sandwiches, drinking out of juice cartons, and playing cards. Patricia hated Hearts, so mostly they played inept poker.

"Is this going to get any more interesting?" Patricia asked at one point.

Gregory and Oscar shook their heads.

"Great," Patricia said grumpily. Then she slouched down to deal another hand of cards. "Aces wild, boys. Place your bets."

They waited and waited, but the dog never showed up. They had stayed so long that the batteries in Gregory's portable tape deck were running down.

"Is it OK if we go now?" Patricia asked. "I'm *really* tired of playing cards."

"Me, too," Oscar confessed.

"We might as well," Gregory said with a sigh. He was pretty sick of cards, too. "I don't think he's coming." He reached for a small plastic bag and started collecting all of their rubbish. "Do you think Mum and Dad would let us come here at night? Maybe we'd find him here, asleep."

"They wouldn't let us come *alone*," Patricia

said. "But if we asked really nicely, they might come with us. I mean, they're the ones who are always telling us to be kind to animals, right?"

Gregory nodded. His parents had always *stressed* the importance of being kind to animals.

"You should write down what you're going to say first," Oscar advised them. He never really liked to leave things to chance. In the Cub Scouts, he had learned a lot about being prepared. "That way, you can practise how you're going to do it. Work out all the problems."

"Let me write it," Patricia told her brother. "I have a bigger vocabulary."

Gregory just shrugged. All he wanted to do was find the dog – one way or another.

He was beginning to be afraid that the dog didn't *want* to be found.

Hours passed before the dog regained consciousness. It was well past midnight, and the woods were pitch-black. His shoulder had stiffened so much that at first, he couldn't get up. But finally, he staggered to his feet. He wanted to lie right back down, but he made himself stay up.

He stood there, swaying. He felt dizzy and sick. What he wanted right now, more than anything, was to be inside that warm cardboard box, sleeping on those soft towels that smelled so clean and fresh.

He limped out to the road, whimpering every time his bad leg hit the ground. The bleeding had stopped, but now that he was moving around, it started up again.

The only way he was going to make it back to the school was if he put one foot in front of the other. He limped painfully up the road, staring down at his front paws the whole way. One step. Two. Three. Four. It was hard work.

Whenever possible, he took shortcuts. He cut through alleys, and car parks, and backyards. The lights were off all over town. People were sound asleep, dreaming about Christmas morning. The dog just staggered along, putting one foot in front of the other. Over and over.

He was plodding through someone's front

yard when he felt the hair on his back rise. Oh, now what? He was *too tired*. But – he smelled smoke! Even though he was dizzy, he lifted his head to sniff the air. Where was it coming from?

He followed the trail across several yards and up to a yellow two-storey house. Smoke was billowing out through a crack in the living room window. Someone had left the Christmas tree lights on, and the tree had ignited! The lights were snapping and popping, and the ornaments were bursting into flames. He could hear the crackle of electricity, and smell the smoke getting stronger.

The house was on fire!

He lurched up the front steps and on to the porch. He was too weak to paw on the door, but he *could* still bark. He threw his head back and howled into the silent night. He barked and barked until the other dogs in the neighbourhood woke up and started joining in. Soon, there were dogs howling and yapping everywhere.

After a few minutes of that, lights started going on in houses up and down the block.

The dog was losing strength, but he kept barking. Why didn't the people come outside? Didn't they know that their house was burning?

The living room windows were becoming black from the smoke, as the fire spread. Why wouldn't the people wake up? Maybe he was going to have to go in and *get* them. But, how?

He started throwing his body feebly against the front door, but it wouldn't budge. Why couldn't the people hear him barking? Where were they? If they didn't wake up soon, they might die from the smoke!

The dog limped to the farthest end of the porch, trying to gather up all of his strength. Then he raced towards the living room window and threw himself into the glass at full speed. The window shattered and he landed in the middle of the burning room. He was covered with little shards of glass, but he didn't have time to shake them off. He had to go and find the family! The floor was very hot, and he burned the bottom of his paws as he ran across the room. It was scary in here!

The doorway was blocked by fire, but he

launched himself up into the air and soared through the flames. He could smell burned fur where his coat had been singed, but he ignored that and limped up the stairs as fast as he could. He kept barking and howling the entire way, trying to sound the alarm. A burning ember had fallen on to his back and he yelped when he felt the pain, but then he just went back to barking.

A man came stumbling out of the master bedroom in a pair of flannel pyjamas. It was Mr Brown, who lived in the house with his wife and two daughters, and he was weak from smoke inhalation.

"Wh-what's going on?" Mr Brown mumbled. "It's the middle of the –"

The dog barked, and tugged at his pyjama leg with his teeth, trying to pull him down the stairs.

Mr Brown saw the flames downstairs and gasped. "Fire!" he yelled, and ran into his children's bedroom. "Wake up, everyone! The house is on fire!"

The dog ran into the master bedroom, barking as loudly as he could until Mrs

Brown groggily climbed out of bed. She was coughing from the smoke, and seemed very confused. The dog barked, and nudged her towards the door.

Mr Brown rushed down the stairs with his two sleepy children and a squirming Siamese cat, and then went back for his wife. By now, she was only steps behind him, carrying a cage full of gerbils.

The dog was exhausted, but he kept barking until they were all safely outside. Once he was sure the house was empty, he staggered out to the yard, his lungs and eyes hurting from the thick smoke. He sank down in the snow, coughing and gagging and quivering from fear.

One of the neighbours had called 911, and the first fire engine was just arriving. The firefighters leaped out, carrying various pieces of equipment and grabbing lengths of hose. By now, the fire had spread from the living room to the dining room.

"Is anyone still in there?" the engine company lieutenant yelled.

"No," Mrs Brown answered, coughing

from the smoke she had inhaled. "It's OK! We all got out."

Because they had been called only a minute or two after the fire started, the fire department was able to put the fire out quickly. Although the living room and dining room were destroyed, the rest of the house had been saved. Instead of losing everything, including their lives, the Browns would still have a place to live.

During all of this, the dog had limped over to the nearest bush. He crawled underneath it as far as he could go. Then he collapsed in exhaustion. His injured shoulder was throbbing, he was still gagging, and all he could smell was smoke. His paws hurt, and he licked at the pads, trying to get rid of the burning sensation. They hurt so much that he couldn't stop whimpering. His back was stinging from where the ember had hit it, and he had lots of new cuts from leaping through the glass. He huddled into a small ball, whimpering to himself. He had never been in so much pain in his life.

While the other firefighters checked to

make sure that the fire was completely out, the chief went over to interview Mr and Mrs Brown. The Oceanport Fire Department was staffed by volunteers, and Fire Chief Jefferson had run the department for many years.

"How did you get out?" Chief Jefferson asked, holding an incident report form and a ballpoint pen. "Did your smoke detector wake you up?"

Mr and Mrs Brown exchanged embarrassed glances.

"We, um, kind of took the battery out a few days ago," Mr Brown mumbled. "See, the remote control went dead, and…" His voice trailed off.

"We were going to get another battery for the smoke detector," Mrs Brown said, coming to his defence. "But, with the holidays and all, we just –"

"Hadn't got round to it yet," Chief Jefferson finished the sentence for her.

The Browns nodded, and looked embarrassed.

Chief Jefferson sighed. "Well, then, all I

can say is that you were very lucky. On a windy night like tonight, a fire can get out of control in no time."

Mr and Mrs Brown and their daughters nodded solemnly. They knew that they had had a very close call.

"So, what happened?" Chief Jefferson asked. "Did you smell the smoke?"

The Browns shook their heads.

"We were all asleep," Mrs Brown said.

Chief Jefferson frowned. "Then I don't understand what happened. Who woke you up?"

The Browns looked at one another.

"It was Santa Paws!" they all said in unison. "Who else?"

Chapter 15

It was Christmas morning, and the Callahans were getting ready to go to church. On Christmas Eve they had gone over to the Oceanport Hospital maternity ward to visit their brand-new niece. Mr Callahan's brother Steve and his wife Emily had had a beautiful baby girl named Miranda. Gregory and Patricia thought she was kind of red and wrinkly, but on the whole, pretty cute.

On the way home, they talked their parents into stopping at the middle school. But when they went to the little alcove, the food and water dishes hadn't been touched. The towels were still neatly folded, too. For some reason, the dog had never returned. Maybe he was gone for good.

Gregory knew that something terrible must have happened to him, but right now, there wasn't anything he could do about it. As far as he knew, no one had seen the dog since he had found Rachel's wallet that morning. And that was *hours* ago. Now, for all Gregory knew, the dog could be lying somewhere, alone, and scared, and *hurt*.

His father put his hand on his shoulder. "Come on, Greg," he said gently. "It'll be OK. We'll come back again tomorrow."

Gregory nodded, and followed his family back to the car.

They went home and ate cookies and listened to Christmas carols. Mrs Callahan made popcorn. Mr Callahan read *The Night Before Christmas* aloud. Patricia told complicated jokes, and Gregory pretended that he thought they were funny. Then they all went to bed.

Gregory didn't get much sleep. He was too upset. Deep inside, he knew that the dog was gone for good. He was sure that he would never see him again – and the thought of that made him feel like crying.

When he got up, even though it was Christmas Day, he was more sad than excited. He and his father both put on suits and ties to wear to church. His mother and Patricia wore long skirts and festive blouses. Patricia also braided red and green ribbons into her hair.

Every year, on Christmas morning, there was a special, non-religious, interdenominational service in Oceanport. No matter what holiday they celebrated, everyone in town was invited. This year, the Mass was being held at the Catholic church, but Rabbi Gladstone was going to be the main speaker. Next year, the service would be at the Baptist church, and the Methodist minister would lead the ceremony. As Father Reilly always said, it wasn't about religion, it was about *community*. It was about *neighbours*.

"Come on, Gregory," Mrs Callahan said as they got into the car. "Cheer up. It's Christmas."

Gregory nodded, and did his best to smile. Inside, though, he was miserable.

"When we get home, we have all those

presents to open," Patricia reminded him. "And I spent *a lot* of money on yours."

Gregory smiled again, feebly.

The church was very crowded. Almost the entire town had shown up. People were smiling, and waving, and shaking hands with each other. There was a definite feeling of goodwill in the air. Oceanport was *always* a friendly and tolerant town, but the holiday season was special.

Gregory sat in his family's pew with his eyes closed and his hands tightly folded. He was wishing with all of his heart that the dog was OK. No matter how hard he tried, he couldn't seem to feel *any* Christmas spirit. How could he believe in the magic of Christmas, if he couldn't even save one little stray dog?

Rabbi Gladstone stepped up to the podium in the front of the church. "Welcome, everyone," he said. "Season's greetings to all of you!"

Then, the service began.

After the fire had been put out and the Browns had gone across the street to stay with neighbours, the dog was alone underneath his bush. He dragged himself deeper into the woods, whimpering softly. He knew he was badly hurt, and that he needed help.

He crawled through the woods until he couldn't make it any further. Then he lay down on his side in the snow. He stayed in that same position all night long. By now, he was too exhausted even to *whimper*.

In the morning, he made himself get up. If he stayed here by himself, he might die. Somehow he had to make it back to the school. If he could do that, maybe his friends Gregory and Oscar would come and help him. He *needed* help, desperately.

Each limping step was harder than the one before, and the dog had to force himself to keep going. The town seemed to be deserted. He limped down Main Street, undisturbed.

The park was empty, too. The dog staggered across the wide expanse, falling down more than once. He was cold, he was in pain and he was *exhausted*.

Naturally, he was also hungry.

When he tottered past the church, he paused at the bottom of the stairs. The doors were open and welcoming, warm air rushed out at him. For days, he had been trying to *give* help. Maybe now it was time to *get* some.

He dragged himself up the steps. His shoulder throbbed and burned with pain the entire way. When he got to the top, he was panting heavily. Could he make it any further, or should he just fall down right here?

He could smell lots of people. Too many people. Too many different scents. Some of the scents were familiar, but he was too confused to sort them all out. *Walking* took up all of his energy.

He hobbled into the church, weaving from sided to side. He started down the centre aisle, and then his bad leg gave out under his weight. He fell on the floor and then couldn't get up again. He let his head slump forward against his front paws and then closed his eyes.

A hush fell over the church.

"I don't believe it," someone said, sounding stunned. "It's Santa Paws!"

Now that the silence had been broken, everyone started talking at once.

Hearing the name "Santa Paws", Gregory

sat up straight in his pew. Then he stood up so he could see better.

"That's my dog," he whispered, so excited that he was barely able to breathe. "Look at my poor dog!" Then he put his fingers in his mouth, and let out – noisy *air*.

Sitting next to him, Patricia sighed deeply. "*Really*, Greg," she said, and shook her head with grave disappointment. "Is that the best you can do?" She sighed again. Then she stuck her fingers in her mouth, and sent out a sharp, clear, and *earsplitting* whistle.

Instantly, the dog lifted his head. His ears shot up, and his tail began to rise.

"That's my dog!" Gregory shouted. He climbed past his parents and stumbled out into the aisle.

The dog was still too weak to get up, but he waved his tail as Gregory ran over to him.

"Are you all right?" Gregory asked, fighting back tears. "Don't worry, I'll take care of you. You're safe now."

Everyone in the church started yelling at once, and trying to crowd around the injured dog.

Patricia lifted her party skirt up a few inches so that she wouldn't trip on it. Then she stepped delicately into the aisle on her bright red holiday high heels.

"Quiet, please," she said in her most commanding voice. Then she raised her hands for silence. "Is there a vet in the house?"

A man and a woman sitting in different sections of the church each stood up.

"Good." Patricia motioned for them both to come forward. "Step aside, please, everyone, and let them through."

A few people did as she said, but there was still a large, concerned group hovering around Gregory and the dog. The vets were trying to get through, but the aisle was jammed.

Patricia's whistle was even more piercing this time. "I *said*," she repeated herself in a no-nonsense voice, "please step aside, in an orderly fashion."

The people standing in the aisle meekly did as they were told.

Watching all of this from their pew, Mr Callahan leaned over to his wife.

"Do you get the sudden, sinking feeling

that someday, we're going to have another cop in the family?" he asked.

Mrs Callahan laughed. "I've had that feeling since she was *two*," she answered.

Gregory waited nervously as the two vets examined the dog.

"Don't worry," the female vet announced after a couple of minutes. "He's going to be just fine."

Her colleague nodded. "Once we get him cleaned up and bandaged, and put in a few stitches, he'll be as good as new!"

Everyone in the church started clapping.

"Hooray for Santa Paws!" someone yelled.

"Merry Christmas, and God bless us every-one!" a little boy in the front row contributed.

Mr Callahan leaned over to his wife again. "If that kid is holding a crutch, I'm *out* of here."

Mrs Callahan grinned. "That's just Nathanial Haversham. His parents are *actors*."

"Oh." Mr Callahan looked relieved. "Good."

Up in the front of the church, Rabbi Gladstone tapped on the microphone to get everyone's attention. Gradually, the church quietened down.

"Thank you," he said. "I think that this week, we've all seen proof that there *can* be holiday miracles. Even when it's hard to believe in magic, wonderful, unexplained things can still happen. That dog – an ordinary dog – has been saving lives and helping people throughout this season." He smiled in the dog's direction. "Thank you, and welcome to Oceanport, Santa Paws!"

Gregory didn't want to be rude, but he had to speak up. "Um, I'm sorry, Rabbi, but that's not his name," he said shyly.

"Whew," Patricia said, and pretended to wipe her arm across her forehead. "Promise me you're not going to call him Brownie, or Muffin, or anything else *cute*."

Gregory nodded. If he came up with a cute name, his sister would never let him live it down. Somehow, the name would have to be *cool*.

"What *is* his name, son?" Rabbi Gladstone asked kindly from the podium.

Gregory blinked a few times. His mind was

a complete blank. "Well, uh, it's uh –"

"Sparky!" Oscar shouted, sitting with his family several rows away.

Everyone laughed.

"It's *not* Sparky," Gregory assured them. "It's, uh –"

"Solomon's a very nice name," Rabbi Gladstone suggested. "Isaiah has a nice ring to it, too."

Now, everyone in the church started shouting out different ideas. Names like Hero, and Rex, and Buttons.

"Oh, yeah, *Buttons*," Patricia said under her breath. "Like we wouldn't be totally humiliated to have a dog named *Buttons*."

Other names were suggested. Champ, and Sport, and Dasher, and Dancer. Frank, and Foxy, and Bud.

Bud?

Gregory looked at his dog for a long time. The dog wagged his tail and then lifted his paw into his new owner's lap. Gregory thought some more, and then, out of nowhere, it came to him. After all, what was another name for Santa Claus?

"His name's Nicholas," he told everyone. Then he smiled proudly and shook his dog's paw. "We call him *Nick*."

The dog barked and wagged his tail.

Then, Gregory stood up. "Come on, Nicky," he said. "It's time to go home."

The dog got up, too, balancing on three legs. He wagged his tail as hard as he could, and pressed his muzzle into Gregory's hand. He had a new owner, he had a new home, and he was going to have a whole new life.

He could hardly wait to get started!